Virginia

Inches Away,

Worlds Apart

Chapter One

2008

Grace was a bit fed up with being in the net-ball team. She was adequate in the position of goal attack, enough to prevent her being thrown out of the team, but didn't particularly enjoy it, however, if she endured the torture of practice she would be able to walk home with her best friend Jenny, who was, frankly, brilliant at any sport.

Net-ball practice was on Thursdays after school and, once it was over Grace and Jenny would chat as they walked, until they reached the top of Leasowe Road where they went their separate ways home.

It was February and freezing. Grace's grand plan for the evening was tea, homework, Eastenders and then probably more telly. She would be glad when the weather was better and she could go out with her friends in the evenings.

Her mum didn't like her being out in the dark and, to be honest, Grace didn't much like the cold.

On today's journey home, Grace and Jenny started gossiping about their friend, Louise. Louise had been taken by her rich Aunty Sue to a really posh hairdressers in Liverpool for her birthday. She had a restyle which had cost more than sixty pounds (her aunt wasn't really rich but she had no children of her own and so was fairly flush).

" I don't really think it suits her," said Jenny. Grace knew that Jenny was jealous and that Louise's hair was fab. She was, in fact, herself jealous of the layers in Louise's thick hair which seemed to sit so beautifully around her face, unlike Grace's which seemed to stick out at every opportunity. Grace wished her mum and dad could afford to send her somewhere posh to have her hair done.

Grace was sure one day she would become be rich. Hours of practice in front of the mirror singing and dancing meant that she would soon be good enough to compete with the likes of Miley Cyrus or Beyonce, after all, she knew all the moves and the words to all their songs, but until the day she was discovered she would have to remain fairly poor.

She had toyed with the idea of having an expensive hair style as part of her birthday present but she had desperately needed an iPod which absolutely wouldn't wait until the following Christmas, she had also wanted to go shopping for clothes with any money she got from various grandparents, aunts and uncles, so the hair would have to be done at her usual, adequate, but unexciting hairdressers, where despite what grace asked for, or the image she had in her head, her hairdresser would generally replicate the style of her previous visit.

The two girls were stood at the top of Leasowe Road as they usually did and carried on talking as though they hadn't seen each other for weeks.

They discussed the fact that Mrs Chapman was probably the most evil teacher that there had ever been, due to the fact that she had separated Grace and Jenny for talking in class, after asking them to 'please be quiet' several times first, and also because she had confiscated Jenny's phone because she was texting during an important lesson on the second world war, (well, Mrs Chapman thought it was an important lesson on the second world war, the girls most definitely did not).

The girls also decided that Mr Dunn, their maths teacher, could be quite fanciable if only he didn't wear those awful 'old man's shoes and jacket'. Mr Dunn was pretty ancient... at least thirty years old.

After these vital topics had been fully discussed Grace made the first move to go as it was so cold, could barely feel her toes. She had won the battle with her mother about which shoes to buy. Grace's mother thought the ballet-like shoes Grace insisted on having, and that all her friends had, were 'ridiculous' for the winter. To avoid proving her right, she could never complain to her mother about her cold feet and would change into her pink fluffy slippers the minute she got in.

Grace had saved some of her dinner money to buy some sweets on the way home. She would buy a bag of millions to eat while she was watching 'Easties' and hoped that her brother James wasn't around so she didn't have to share them with him. Her mother always said it was nice to share but Grace didn't think that this was always the case and couldn't see any benefit in giving any of her sweets to a brother who tormented her at every opportunity.

Grace didn't care much for James most of the time, although she did quite fancy his friend, Nathan, not that she would admit this to anyone, least of all, James. She was very conscious of how she behaved when Nathan was around, she didn't want James catching on, or her life would be hell. Anyway, Nathan was fifteen and Grace was only thirteen, she was just a little girl to him, so she would just dream of the day he would realise that she was the only girl for him. She imagined the scenario when Nathan would knock on the door and Grace would answer, she would offer to fetch James but Nathan would say that he had actually come to see her, he would take her by the hand and lead her to the park (she would have to make sure she had her shoes on at this point, pink fluffy slippers she felt would spoil the moment) he would buy her ice cream and they would sit under an old oak tree (or any other type of tree would do) and then he would kiss her and declare his undying love for her.

Grace snapped out of her recurring day dream as approached the sweet shop which stood on the corner after Leasowe Road just near the video shop. She fished out the money from the inside pocket of her blazer. Sixty five pence, enough for her bag of millions.

Big decision of the day now, blue or pink millions? Grace took longer than usual to decide. Some decisions are just too important to rush. Grace bought her millions and opened the bag as she walked out of the door of the shop, she had chosen pink ones, next time she would definitely have blue.

The sweet shop was just before the pelican crossing where Grace's mother insisted she cross the road. The road through Wallasey Village was a busy one and she could hear her mum say 'I don't want a phone call from the hospital thank you very much'. Whenever they where out together, Grace's mother would always ask Grace if she wanted to press the button to summon the green man, Grace always did, she didn't have the heart to tell her mother that it wasn't quite the most exciting part of her day, as she wasn't five anymore. This always made her smile when she was on her own and she would always politely check that there weren't actually any five year olds around who would enjoy the experience much more than she

She would just have a few of the pink delights on the way home and then save the rest for when she was watching telly later. She tilted her head back and dropped a handful of the sweets into her mouth spilling a few as she did. As she lowered her head she felt a strangeness about her and in front of her she saw a very old car, like the ones she had seen in her granddad's photographs. Grace stared at the old car as she walked the few steps to the crossing, things just didn't feel right.

She looked up to press the button to summon the green man.

Grace stepped forward to press the button, still staring at the old car.

"Oh my god!" she muttered under her breath. No button to press, no crossing, no school on the opposite side of the road, everything different and yet familiar at the same time.

Graces stomach seemed to flip over, she froze and held her breath in panic. 'What the hell was going on?' she thought. Grace closed her eyes for a second and opened them hoping for normality. The road had changed, the shops were different there were very few cars but they were all old like the first one she had seen, and yet some of them looked shiny and new. Grace's mind raced. The only explanation she could come up with was that someone was making a film here, stupid really, as why would they knock down a whole school, and why didn't she notice it before. Grace couldn't think of any other explanation and before she could take in any more of her surroundings she ran back into the shop in a uneasy panic to ask the shopkeeper what was going on outside. She was bound to have an explanation. The shopkeeper followed Grace out, hungry for some excitement to disrupt her humdrum day, the most exciting part so far was someone winning ten pounds on the previous nights lottery, not too thrilling, but the elderly lady who had the winning ticket had been quite elated had bought a bag of mint imperials to celebrate.

Grace stepped out, her heart still pounding, and saw the usual pelican crossing, the usual school and the usual cars. The shopkeeper looked around in anticipation, Grace was mortified. She apologised and said she thought she saw something. The shopkeeper muttered something under her breath about hormones and went back inside to her warm shop.

Grace continued her journey home with the image in her head, completely perplexed, and wondered how she could have imagined it all.

Chapter 2

1920

Flo had quite a good day in school. Her first lesson of the morning was cookery with Miss Woods. They had all made a Victoria sponge cake, which Flo would take home for tea. Hers had risen beautifully and was a vast improvement on the last, slightly more biscuity one which her family had eaten without criticism. Next she had the usual daily arithmetic. Flo always found this quite easy and knew all her times tables off by heart. Her teacher Miss Gardener often complemented Flo on her ability and neatness, whilst poor Elizabeth Thompson was often kept after school for her blotchy work and poor handwriting. Flo felt really sorry for her, it didn't seem to matter how hard she tried poor Elizabeth never seemed to be able to please Miss Gardener. Elizabeth, was fortunate to have a teacher as kind as Miss Gardener who did not like to punish her pupils physically, however, on the odd occasion when Miss Gardener was unwell the class had been taken by the head mistress, who would hit any of the girls on the wrist with a ruler for the slightest misdemeanour. Elizabeth generally got the lions share of this punishment and was even hit one day because she had banged down the lid of her desk too loudly. Flo was terrified of the woman.

Before lunch the class had spent an hour reading in silence. Flo was reading The Secret Garden by Frances Hodgson Burnett. A story about a young girl called Mary, who, after the death of her parents is brought back to England from India to live with her uncle, where she discovers a secret garden. Flo found the story very engrossing and would imagine herself as Mary as she read.

After lunch Flo had attended her typing class. This was her downfall and the lesson that she dreaded most. She couldn't seem to get her fingers to work quickly enough and could only manage a measly fifteen words a minute. Catherine Dixon could already do thirty-five words a minute. Flo would pretend she didn't care. She didn't want to be a secretary anyway, she wanted to be a teacher, like Miss Gardener, who was very pretty, kind and idolised by Flo.

The final lesson of the day was P.E. and the class went out to play rounders. Flo loved the game but it was freezing outside, the snow had only recently melted. She hoped she would warm up after running around, but was caught out on her first bat by Gillian Wood and so by the time she came to field she felt she had already turned to ice despite jumping from one foot to the other and holding her hands under her arm pits.

The opportunity for a good run around came when Hannah Donnelly hit the ball right to the other end of the yard and had got to fourth base before Flo had even picked up the ball, despite warming her up ever so slightly, Flo was not impressed with the smug look on Hannah's face. Flo wasn't a violent person but she thought that Hannah had the face that deserved to be slapped on occasion.

Flo arrived home that afternoon and proudly presented the Victoria sponge to her mother before warming herself by the lovely hot fire, which her mother always made sure was roaring during the winter months for when hor children came home.

'That looks delicious, Flo" said her mother.

"Can we have some now, pleeease" pleaded George, Flo's younger and annoying brother.

"Certainly not" replied their mother,

"We will save it for after tea"

Flo's mother employed a maid called Alice to help her with the daily chores and Alice was given every Thursday afternoon off (as well as every Sunday), making Thursday the day that Flo's mother made dinner for the family. A chore she quite enjoyed. It was also one of the days that Flo was sent down to the bakers for some fresh bread to have with their dinner. Flo didn't mind at all even though she had only just got warm, as she was always given a penny to buy sweets, a weekly treat for her and George.

She took the money for the bread and the penny for sweets and made her way, as usual, down to the shops in the village. She would walk down Grove Road and cut through St. George's Road to Sandy Lane. She would then walk through the village to the sweet shop first before making her way to Broomes bakery for the bread.

Flo loved the smell of the shop, the mixture of smells from the tobacco and the numerous jars of sweets that lined the shelves. She always took her time in choosing her weekly treat as if prolonging the anticipation. George always wanted toffees.

Mrs Powell, the well-rounded shopkeeper, was always happy to see Flo. She found her to be 'a very polite young lady and a credit to her parents, the Doctor and Mrs Renshaw'.

Mrs Powell was always very polite and respectful to anyone with any social standing in the community and as Flo's father was a doctor of medicine he and his family deserved her extra special attention. Mrs Powell also managed to communicate beautifully in the Kings English when speaking to such people, although her use of language would have shocked Flo had she been present an hour earlier when she was screaming at her son, Jim, for not cleaning out the store room to the standard his mother expected.

"How is your mother after her illness? I have been extremely worried about her" enquired Mrs Powell,

Flo's mother had suffered with a heavy cold over the past week but had soldiered on as usual.

"Much better thank you" replied Flo.

Flo's mother was very hard working and although Alice was there to keep on top of things, kept her house clean and tidy, beyond necessity, Flo thought.

After much deliberation, Flo finally chose some barley twists. Mrs Powell weighed out a quarter of the sweets on the scales with the little weights on, adding a couple more as she usually did. Flo smiled knowingly, she always got a little extra although she never dared expect it. She would share the sweets with her friend Will with whom she hoped to meet up with later once she had finished her chores which included setting the table for dinner and her piano practice (most definitely a chore). Flo knew that if she could finished the chores before tea she would have more time afterwards to meet Will. They would often walk up to the Breck which was a small hill with trees, behind which was a clearing, ideal for playing in. They would meet with some of the other children from both of their schools. They would play a variety of games including football, cricket, skipping. Sometimes they would ride their bikes and some of the children even had roller skates. There was never much time in the winter months and they would play near one of the big houses which was well lit so they could see a little better. The children looked forward to the lighter nights so that they could stay out longer and could at least see the ball they were playing with. There was always much more to do during the summer months. If the weather was good enough a great deal of the time would be spent on the beach in New Brighton. They would sail their boats at the Captains Pit, (a large pond on Hoeside Road), which is said to be aptly named after a sea captain, who's wife had drowned herself in the pond after hearing that her husband had drowned at sea. Flo thought this story was very sad and hoped it wasn't true.

Boats were bought, usually as birthday or Christmas presents and some were home made. They would look for birds nests or just climb the trees for the fun of it. The boys would also enjoy looking for and often torturing various insects, a sport Flo found cruel and particularly gruesome. Sometimes they would go fruit picking, not strictly legal, but an acceptable crime in the eyes of the children and the luxury of a freshly baked apple pie would be enjoyed by their respective families over the following couple of days. One of Flo's favourite games was 'what's the time Mr Wolf' which she considered herself to be particularly good at, she could be very nimble and quiet when creeping up on whoever was 'on'.

Whichever game was chosen, one thing was sure, they always had great fun and on the whole went home considerably more dirty and tired than when they came out. Flo particularly loved the summers.

Flo thought she might take her long skipping rope out with her later, it would keep them warm, the rope would stretch across Breck Road and was long enough for three people to skip at one time. The boys of course didn't generally want to join in with the skipping and would go off and find something much more exciting to do, such as skidding on long frozen puddles.

Flo thanked Mrs Powell for her generosity and paid for the sweets. She took one last sniff of the shop before opening the door to make her way further up the village to the bakery.

Flo stepped out of the shop and shrieked dropping her sweets on the ground.

What Flo saw was not the world she knew, her breathing became rapid and she trembled with fear. The world went black, as if someone had turned off the sun, and she fell to the floor.

Flo came round seconds later to see the same unfamiliar world before her. What had happened? Why had no one come to help her? As she got back to her feet she saw strange looking cars, buildings, and so many funny looking people. Flo was terrified but mesmerised by the alien scene before her. She composed herself and ran back into the shop, glad of the familiar surroundings, not noticing the bump on her head, which would be sore later.

"Mrs Powell, something strange is happening outside, please come quick", Flo's voice sounded urgent and she looked pale and frightened.

Mrs Powell hurried around the counter and outside looked frantically around searching for the strange happening, but saw nothing unusual.

"What is it child?"

"Everything looked different Mrs Powell, like it was a different world" Flo squeezed her eyes tight shut and open again as if to summon the world she had seen earlier. Mrs Powell smiled at Flo. "I think you need to go home and get warm. I think you may be sickening for something. My sister talked of seeing strange sights when she was struck down with pneumonia. Now, would you like me to ask our Jim, to walk you home?"

Jim was seventeen and Mrs Powell's only child. He would stare at Flo whenever she came into the shop and make her feel uncomfortable, before Mrs Powell could summon Jim from the back room Flo quickly refused the offer.

"No, I'll be fine thank-you, I'll go straight home".

Flo just wanted to get away. She felt silly and she was worried she was coming down with the same horrible illness Mrs Powell's sister had.

Flo stepped out of the shop into her own familiar world, she looked around once more to reassure herself that all was as it should be and then rushed home completely forgetting about the bread.

Chapter 3

2008

Grace kept thinking about what she had seen on Thursday. It was now Saturday and she and her friend Jenny were going to Liscard, (the local shopping centre), which did not have a great expanse of shopping opportunities, but provided the all important Primark and McDonalds, and the shop that cut keys, which Grace needed to use too often. She didn't seem to be able to keep a key for more than a couple of months.

Grace had only recently been allowed to go into Liscard with her friends and it made her feel very grown up. James was allowed to travel on the train to Liverpool with his friends. She couldn't wait to be old enough for this as there were so many more shops over there.

Grace and Jenny's friend, Alex, had invited them to her birthday party the following day at the bowling alley in New Brighton. Grace had ten pounds left from her birthday money to buy something new to wear.

The girls walked to the shops and headed straight for Primark where Grace chose a green top. Jenny picked out some white jeans and a necklace to match the pink top she had got for Christmas. They then had the inevitable MacDonald's for lunch before wandering around New Look and tormenting the pigeons.

They made their way home through Wallasey Village and as they crossed the top of Leasowe Road Jenny suggested they stop at the sweet shop and get some goodies for later. They often stayed over at each other's house at the weekends. They would watch DVD's talk to their other friends on MSN or Bebo and make up dances to their recently downloaded tracks.

Grace's stomach flipped over at the memory of Thursday's visit to the shop. She went in sheepishly, hoping that the same shopkeeper was not here today.

"Hello hun, how are you feeling?" the familiar voice asked.

"I'm ok thanks," replied Grace, cringing

"I just felt a bit unwell, that's all".

Jenny gave Grace a 'what happened and why don't I know about it ' look.

Grace avoided her gaze and continued looking at the chocolate. They bought their goodies and left the shop and Grace again recalled the vivid images from couple of days earlier.

"What did she mean? When were you ill?" asked Jenny

"It was nothing, I just felt a bit unwell last time I came into the shop." Grace replied curtly,

Grace and Jenny usually shared everything but Grace wasn't yet ready to share this particular incident with her for fear that Jenny would think she was mad.

During the sleepover they ate their goodies and watched High School Musical (for the umpteenth time), singing along to every word and lusting after the Adonis that is, Zac Efron, whom Grace would consider marrying once she was famous, of course Nathan would then be cast aside.

Paul, Jenny's brother (who was fifteen), had gone into Jenny's room and stole a couple of their strawberry laces without asking.

"Give them back and get out now" Jenny shouted. As Paul stood in the doorway, he smiled and ceremoniously fed both of the strawberry laces into his mouth, just to maximise the level of annoyance. When he felt his work was done, he left and went to his room to watch his own choice of DVD 'Alien Versus Predator'.

The girls slept 'til ten thirty the next morning. Jenny's mum made them pancakes for breakfast with a generous topping of Nutella and banana. They then went back to Grace's house to get ready for the party. This was a very time consuming routine and involved hair straightening, admiring themselves and each other in their new clothes and the application of discreet make-up, apparently invisible to anyone in a parental capacity!

The girls had a great time at the party. Jenny got the second highest score beaten only by Alex's older brother. Typical, thought Grace, does she have to be good at everything. Grace was just glad she managed to get a higher score than Alex's eight year old sister, it was a close call but Alex's sister did have the side barriers up and so had a distinct advantage.

The dreaded Monday morning loomed.

Grace didn't mind school but hated getting up early and thought that it would be much better if lessons started at around 11am. The weekly routine started. Monday evenings off, Tuesdays trampolining, Wednesdays dancing and the usual, (just bearable) netball on Thursdays. All this and homework as well, into which Grace put minimal effort if she was honest. She couldn't really see the point of it.

It was particularly cold walking home this week, although the evenings were getting lighter. Grace made her usual visit to the sweet shop after leaving Jenny to go her way. She needed some comfort sweets after hearing the devastating news that the gorgeous Nathan had asked out one of the girls in year nine who had accepted his kind offer of a date at the cinema. Relieved to see a different shopkeeper this time, Grace chose a bag of Haribo to eat later. She put them into her school bag so that she was not tempted to open them and eat them on the way home.

Grace stepped out of the shop and gasped as she saw the same scene that had greeted her a week earlier. Slightly less fearful than the previous week Grace stood, holding her breath, hardly daring to move. She looked around her. It was as though she had gone back in time. There was a cycle and motor store where the small block of shops with the pizza shop usually stood, there was no sign of the ever expanding catholic high school, but in it's place a building contractors and property repair shop on the corner of Sandy Lane. She looked behind her to find a variety of shops, but not the ones she had usually seen. There were shops all the way along the road where houses usually stood. The cars were all old like the ones she had seen in her granddads photographs. A lady approached wearing a black fur coat with a white fur collar and large buttons which Grace thought was vile, she also wore a matching fur hat, equally vile. Grace felt a wave of bravery and decided to ask her what was going on.

"Excuse me, could you..." but the lady walked straight past and ignored her,

"How rude" muttered Grace.

"Manners cost nothing" Grace then realised she sounded like her mother and gave a shudder. A man then walked towards the shop, he was wearing a long coat and flat hat.

"Excuse me" she spoke a little louder this time. Again she was ignored. What was wrong with these people?

Grace then saw a girl dressed even more strangely than the lady in fur. She wore a long grey coat with an even longer skirt showing below it and some laced black boots, she also wore a beret over her very short but wavy hair. Grace thought she looked like something from one of the telly programmes about olden days that her mother liked to watch. The young girl looked even more terrified than Grace.

"Excuse me!" she tried for the third time, exasperated.

"Hello" replied the young girl.

Chapter 4

1920

Flo awoke the next morning after her 'funny turn' with trepidation. She got out of bed wondering if she would feel unwell, expecting to be struck down with the pneumonia that had apparently killed Mrs Powell's sister. A fact Flo had learned from her mother the evening before.

Flo found that she actually felt rather well, despite the vivid memory of the vision she had seen the day before. She dismissed it as a strange dream but wondered how a person could dream of things they had never seen before. She closed her eyes and tried to visualise the scene again. The way the cars had looked, the clothes that people were wearing. She wished she had taken a lot more time to look around, but fear had overcome her.

Flo continued with her day, not looking forward to her piano lesson after school with the dreadful Miss Cranbourne, who would poke Flo in the arm with her pencil every time Flo played a wrong note or held her hands incorrectly. She certainly couldn't share the passion Miss Cranbourne expressed for the wonderful part to be played by the left hand which was scattered with arpeggios.

Saturday morning brought the sun out and although it was still chilly it felt like spring was finally on its way.

Flo dressed quickly and hurriedly ate the bread and scrambled eggs that Alice had put in front of her. Flo's father looked over the top of his paper and said.

"You will become unwell if you eat so quickly Flo, now slow down or you will spend the day at home reading" Flo looked at her father, smiled and ate as slowly as she could.

Her father tutted and went back to reading his paper. George giggled at Flo's attempt at slow motion eating and then joined in.

Flo finally managed to leave the house with the promise that she would not be too late back.

The Renshaw family had been invited to supper with that evening Mr and Mrs Williams, who lived up the road from Flo. Flo would be expected to recite her latest piano pieces and she would have to endure the excruciating sound of Elsie Williams violin playing. Elsie was Mr and Mrs Williams sixteen year old daughter who Flo found quite annoying at times. She acted as though she was so much older than her sixteen years and she shook her head at every opportunity as if to show off the perfect ringlets hanging around her ugly face. Well, that was Flo's opinion, which differed from her mothers, who seemed to sing Elsie's praises at every opportunity.

Flo intended to have as much fun as possible today to make up for the dreadful evening ahead as she skipped along to Wills house.

Will was waiting for her. He too, had been admonished by his father that morning because he had spilt a full jug of milk over the breakfast table, and then, as he jumped up to avoid it dripping onto him he knocked into his little sister Margaret who then howled for an unnecessarily length of time.

Will and Flo, both relieved to be out, made their way to the Breck to see which of their friends were out.

This was the highest part of the village on which had been built some very imposing houses, such as, Darley Dene and Mosslands. You could see quite far into the distance, across the market gardens and to the river Mersey over to the right. The children played cricket for a good couple of hours. Joe Sanders, Will's friend, had received a brand new cricket set for his birthday and wanted

41

to try it out. The decision was then made to go down to the beach at New Brighton.

They walked past the Cheshire Cheese public house and when they had passed the Black Horse inn, where several of the local men would congregate for a lunchtime pint, Will challenged Flo to a race from the top of Leasowe road to the bottom of Grove road, a distance of approximately half a mile.

Flo ran as fast as she could, Will occasionally would turn around while still running and laugh at the distance he had managed to put between them. Flo still tried her best and was relieved as she passed the Cosmo picture palace and was running through the arcade of shops towards Grove road. She panted, barely able to speak. Will was stood with hands on hips as if he had been waiting there for hours.

"Girls are really no good at running" he laughed.

Flo pulled tongues at him. Her mother would not have pleased to see her tearing down the road at speed with her skirt pulled up almost to her knees, nor pulling tongues, it was not at all ladylike.

Will had been given a penny to spend by his father, luckily it was safely in Wills possession before the milk incident.

They walked passed the New Brighton tower and along the Ham and Egg parade where Will bought them both a currant bun. They sat on the pier eating their buns watching the world go by before meeting up with their friends near Fort Perch Rock, a large fort with drawbridge built in 1826 as a coastal defence battery to defend the port of Liverpool during the Napoleonic wars. The sun had brought a great many people out today, but no-one yet daring to dip their toes in the icy cold waters of the river Mersey.

Flo had a great day but now dreaded the thought of the boring evening ahead which was fast approaching.

The evening arrived and more than fulfilled all her expectations. Elsie had played a particularly tedious rendition of one of Chopin's more well known pieces, of which Flo wouldn't have been able to recall the title, even if her life depended on it, after which both sets of parents gushed about her talent. Flo smiled and told her how lovely it was, while she imagined hitting Elsie over the head with her own violin. Flo really wasn't a violent person but some acts she felt should be permitted in polite society and this one far outweighed slapping Hannah Donnelly's face. The next few days followed a fairly normal routine.

Flo took her usual trip to the bakers and sweet shop on Thursday. Mrs Powell was pleased to see her up and about and with a very concerned look on her face told Flo that she had been worried sick all week about her. Flo thanked her for her concern and reassured her that she had been her usual self since her 'turn' and had no ill affects afterwards.

Flo feeling slightly embarrassed quickly chose a Cadbury's dairy milk bar to eat later and the usual toffees for George, she gave a cursory quick smile to Jim, just to be polite before she left. His smile in return made Flo shudder just a little.

Jim's creepy smile soon faded from her thoughts, as she stepped out of the shop and was met with the scene she had tried so hard to recall several times that week.

Flo managed to compose herself and tried to take some deep breaths, although her heart was beating so loudly she was sure other people would be able to hear it.

Flo's mouth was dry as she looked around at the sight before her, her feet felt as though they were glued to the ground. She was determined not to faint this time and looked back at the shop for some reassurance. Even the shop had changed. This felt very real, and as terrified as Flo was, she wanted to know what was going on. She looked around slowly trying to take in every detail. There were lots of strange looking motorcars. The roads were smooth and seemed much wider. The Travellers Rest was no longer there. In its place was a building contractor. The smooth road was hectic and busy with people, cars and buses. The cars and buses seemed to be travelling quite fast and effortlessly.

She didn't know where to look next. The cars were also smooth looking to match the roads and there were people on shiny bicycles riding past.

The people were wearing such unusual clothes, the woman had short dresses, skirts and coats, which didn't even cover their knees and some were even wearing trousers. Some had their hair really high up on their heads and others had the ends of their hair neatly curling outwards, which Flo thought looked particularly bizarre.

The men generally seemed to be wearing suits, long coats and mainly flat caps. Flo then saw a woman wearing a beautiful long coat made of fur with a matching hat, Flo watched her walk by thinking how warm (and rich) she must have been.

Flo couldn't imagine what had happened to her, was she going mad? Being carted off to the local lunatic asylum wasn't a pleasant thought. The colour drained from Flo's face and she was frozen with fear hardly daring to breathe or move and not knowing what to do next when a young girl spoke to her.

"Excuse me" the young girl said.

"Hello". Replied Flo.

Chapter 5

1964

Grace was relieved somebody had finally acknowledged her.

"Excuse me but could you tell me what's going on?" she asked.

Flo gave a short burst of nervous laughter.

Grace thought that Flo was making fun of her and scowled.

Flo answered.

"I have no idea but it's quite terrifying".

Grace, although terrified herself felt that she should be sensible and grown up. The poor girl looked even more frightened than she did, if that were possible.

"Don't worry, we'll ask someone else".
Grace and Flo stood side by side both glancing at each others strange clothes.

Grace had seen the sort of clothes Flo was wearing before but only in the history books and films that her mother liked to watch.

Flo had never seen anything like Grace's clothes. She thought her short skirt quite inappropriate and she had certainly never seen a young girl wearing a tie before, but she loved her hair, unusual though it was, shaped beautifully around her face and very shiny.

They both smiled not wanting to offend each other by mentioning their respective attire.
A gentleman was walking towards them.

"Excuse Me," said Grace.

"Excuse us, sir," added Flo, respectful, but a little louder, the man walked straight past.

"I've already tried to speak to a few people" Grace explained to Flo "but you are the only one who has taken any notice of me".

They tried to attract the attention of several more people but to no avail.

People were just walking by, minding their own business as if everything was perfectly normal. Grace wanted to scream at them. This was far from normal.

Grace couldn't believe what she was thinking: could anybody actually see them? Flo was coming to the same conclusion as tears rolled down her face.

"They can't see us can they? What has happened to us, do you think we are ghosts?" Grace gasped and choked back the tears

"Do you think we have died?"

Grace tried to recall whether she had come out of the shop and tried to cross the road, maybe she had not summoned the little green man and had been run over. No, she wouldn't do that, what would her mother say.

Would this be the day her mother 'got a phone call from the hospital?'

"There must be another explanation" she replied praying that death wasn't the answer here.

"Anyway, I saw the same thing last week when I came out of the shop and when I went back in everything was normal again".

Flo was taken aback with this news and felt slightly relieved that Grace had shared the same experience.

"Me too, only I fainted" she said feeling quite silly.

"I managed to get back into the shop, Mrs Powell gave me some smelling salts and everything was just as it should be, I thought I was going mad, Mrs Powell thought I was ill, but I felt fine afterwards".

"Well, maybe we are both mad" replied Grace, wondering what smelling salts were.

"Do you suppose if we go back into the shop everything will return to normal again?" Flo asked Grace, as if Grace would have all the answers.

Both girls stood in silence for a few seconds and both were torn between the prospect of returning to normality and the curiosity of their current surroundings.

The girls would have surely chosen the former had they been alone, but having an ally gave them the courage to want to stay a little longer and explore.

"My name is Florence by the way, Florence Elizabeth Renshaw, but everyone calls me Flo"

"I'm Grace, Grace Olivia Bailey" she replied, copying the formalities, "Everyone calls me Grace, except my brother who calls me an idiot."

"Pleased to meet you, your brother sounds delightful," said Flo joining in with the humour.

"It's as though we've just stepped into the past, Flo, look at the old clothes and the cars, my granddad used to have cars like these.

"Well, I've never seen cars like these, there are so many of them, and they drive very fast, and I don't mean to be rude but you and all the ladies I have seen are showing their knees".

To Flo, this could only be the future, if that were possible.

"Flo, what year is this?" asked Grace.

"It's 1920".

Grace gasped again,

"But Flo it's 2008"

The girls stared at each other in disbelief.

"Am I in your world? Is this 2008? This is unbelievable". 2008 didn't even sound like real year to Flo.

"Well, it doesn't look like 2008 to me" replied Grace

The possibility was dawning on Grace that Flo must have travelled forwards in time and that she had travelled backwards, although the idea was quite absurd and she still wondered if the only reasonable explanation was that they were, in fact, ghosts.

Grace looked around trying not to show Flo that she was welling up again at the thought that she had died when she noticed a newspaper rack hanging on the door of the shop.

"Look Flo, there'll be a date on the newspaper won't there"

Both girls looked together at the Daily Mail on the rack.

3rd March 1964.

"Oh my god!" Grace said slowly.

"What has happened to us?" questioned Flo, who despite the enormity of the situation was a little taken aback at Grace blaspheming so unashamedly.

Grace didn't know whether to be excited or scared.

"We seemed to have travelled in time, you know, like Doctor Who, but without the tardis".

"Doctor who?" asked Flo.

The old knock knock joke that her granddad still told sprang to mind but Grace quickly realised that it was probably inappropriate under the present circumstances.

"Never mind, just someone off the telly"

"The what?" asked Flo

"The television, you know, you don't have a telly?"

"I don't even know what that is"

Grace was stumped. How would she explain that one?

"Doesn't matter." Explaining the wonders of television didn't seem important at the moment but Grace did think it would be awful not to have one.

Grace and Flo looked at each other not sure what to do or say next, both feeling drawn by the shop, wondering if they could really get back home, but not wanting to miss out on this strange but exciting opportunity

"Do you live far?" asked Flo

"No, just up Sandy Lane"

"That's not far, I live on Sea Road, I was just on my way home, well, I was just going to the bakers to buy some bread for tea first ".

"Yeah, I'm just off home too, I was playing netball after school and came into the shop to buy some sweets".

The conversation seemed trivial under the circumstances but the girls really did not know what to say.

"Mum will probably start to worry soon if I don't get home but it would be a shame not to spend some more time with you and see how things looked in the past." Said Grace.

"Or the future" laughed Flo.

"This is so weird, Flo." Grace wanted to check the time. The girls had no idea how long they had been here.

Grace fished in her school bag for her phone. It was a new pink Samsung she had got for Christmas. Grace had loved it at first but the novelty was wearing off and she had already scratched the screen.

"Oh my word! Is that a watch from the future?" asked Flo.

"No, it's my phone but it does have the time on it".

"A phone! A telephone! How can it…..?" Flo wasn't sure what to ask.

"It's a mobile phone, it works anywhere, well almost anywhere". Remembering the trauma of her holiday in Wales last year when she couldn't get a signal on her old phone unless she climbed a nearby mountain, which incidentally, she did not.

"Can I see it?" Flo asked excitedly.

"Yeah, sure" Grace handed the phone to Flo who held it as if it were a precious stone.

"How does it work?"

Grace felt a powerful responsibility to educate this young girl from the past on the wonders of modern science, but then, she actually had no clue how it did work.

Grace found, not surprisingly, that she had no signal.

"Well, I can't ring my mum from here," she said with a nervous giggle.

The time on the phone read 16.54, which meant that although it must have been a good half an hour since the girls came out of the shop, no time seemed to have past. They stared at the time for a good while to see if it would change, but it didn't. Grace scrolled through her contacts comforting herself with the familiarity of family and friends and felt an urge to go home.

Flo had so many questions she wanted to ask Grace but she didn't know where to start. She was amazed enough by Graces mobile telephone and wondered what her friend Will would make of it.

Flo and Will had been friends since they could remember, their mothers had been good friends since they where at school. They spent most of there spare time together.

Flo's father was a doctor at a hospital in Liverpool and Will's father was a headmaster at a school in Birkenhead. Neither was rich but both lived a very comfortable life.

Although intrigued by the wonders of this modern world Flo also felt a surge of emotion and a need to go home.

She looked at Grace with tears in her eyes.

"Grace, I'd like to go home,' as if asking permission "but it was lovely to meet you" remembering her manners.

"Me too" said Grace, relieved that Flo had taken the first step for them to attempt their return to normality.

"I wonder if we'll meet again," said Flo

"Maybe we should come into the shop every day and see what happens.

"I wish I could, but I usually only come in on Thursdays and sometimes Saturdays if father asks me to fetch him some tobacco, Mrs Powell would think it strange if I came in every day without buying anything "

"Well, I really hope I meet you again Flo"

Both girls nervously approached the shop door; terrified they would not be able to return home, but sorry to part from each other and this alien world.

"After you Flo" Grace offered politely although she didn't really want to be the one left alone.

Flo opened the door and turned to smile at Grace before entering the shop.

"You back again Flo, did you forget something?" the familiar voice of Mrs Powell made Flo give a big sigh with relief and want to jump over the counter and hug the woman. To find that you are not in fact dead is a wonderful feeling.

"Oh, I thought I'd left my purse, but silly me it's in my pocket"

Mrs Powell tutted 'what is wrong with that girl' she muttered to herself, and made a mental note to keep an eye on her. She felt a great responsibility towards her customers and was quick to tell someone if she thought they looked unwell, indeed, didn't she point out to Mrs Smith last November that she was looking pale and wasn't the poor woman dead within the week. Mrs Powell had been proud that her observation had been correct although it did Mrs Smith no good whatsoever.

Flo looked flustered and pulled her cloth purse out of her pocket as if to prove she had just found it.

She skipped home, remembering to visit the bread shop on her way this time, relieved to be back but so excited about her experience. She wished she could go straight back and meet Grace again and couldn't wait to tell Will about her adventure. She wondered if he would believe her. Maybe she should keep it to herself. Without any proof he would probably think she was mad and the returning thought of being carted off to the lunatic asylum made her think again.

Flo knew that lunatic asylums weren't very nice places to be and although it had become policy after the 1870's for harmless cases to stay in the workhouses and that only the dangerously insane were sent to the asylums, the workhouse was not much of a better option.

Flo would wait and see.

Grace felt the same relief as she found herself in the shop and was accidentally shoved by one of the local boys who was messing about with his mates.

"You boys can come in one at a time if you don't behave" the shopkeeper shouted to them.

The boy apologised sheepishly to Grace, she smiled at him

"It's ok", everything was truly ok at the moment, and she walked out of the shop.

How jealous they would be if they knew of the experience Grace had just had.

Grace felt very special as she walked home and had a great yearning to see Flo again. She tried to recall everything she had seen and now wished she had stayed just a little longer so that she could have taken in more of her surroundings.

Like Flo, Grace also toyed with the idea of telling someone about what had happened, and although she was bursting to share her news, at least with Jenny, she knew it was highly unlikely that anyone would believe her. To have an imaginary friend at the age of thirteen was not going to be considered cool and although she was ninety nine per cent sure she did not imagine Flo, that would not be the opinion of her family and friends and particularly her brother, who would be delighted that Grace had proved that she was indeed, an idiot.

Chapter 6

1920

Flo arrived home and couldn't concentrate on her usual evening routine. She was so excited she didn't feel like eating her tea, even though it was her favourite,... meat pie. Her mother, like Mrs Powell, was also becoming concerned that Flo was unwell or perhaps the other reason for her 'symptoms' was that she had a crush on someone, distracted and off her food, classic signs of being in love. Her mother hoped it was the latter.

The week couldn't pass by quick enough and the normal routine of her life seemed dull in comparison to meeting Grace and seeing some of the wonderful things of the future.

Each time she saw Will she desperately wanted to tell him about it, she knew that he would have particularly loved to see all the modern cars, but each time she had hesitated and decided against it.

Will liked Flo, she was fun, unlike some of the other girls he knew she was happy to climb trees and didn't much care about getting dirty much to the despair of her mother who thought Flo should start acting a little more like a young lady, she was twelve after all

On Sunday, after church, if the weather wasn't too bad they would ask their respective parents if they could go for a walk. Playing out was frowned upon on Sundays, their need for some fresh air was taken with a pinch of salt by their parents, and they were usually allowed out for an hour or two.

Today, Flo wanted to walk through the village. She wanted to stand in the same spot and remember as many details as possible of the area she had seen in 1964.

Flo stood outside the shop and looked out trying to visualise what she had seen two days earlier. She was amazed merely by the difference in the amount of people that would pass by. She stood and counted only eight people that she could see from where she stood. Will stood next to her and looked up and down just as Flo was doing, wondering what she was looking at. Will couldn't see anything remotely interesting and looked at Flo as if to say ' why are we just stood here looking up and down'. Flo smiled at him and desperately wanted to tell him that, one day, in about 90 years time there would be a shop, opposite which would sell pizzas, a food Flo understood to be from Italy and was like a very flat pie with no top. There would be cars speeding past so fast you could barely see them, and you would be able to telephone anyone you liked right here in the middle of the street. Will wasn't enjoying this 'standing staring up the road' game at all.

"Let's go and see who's up on the Breck".

Will was already striding off.

Flo followed like an obedient puppy.

Chapter 7

2008

Grace's week went agonisingly slowly, even though her mum and dad took her and Jenny to the pictures on Sunday, and then to Frankie and Benny's for tea, nothing compared to the short half hour of excitement she had experienced on the previous Thursday.

Grace clock watched in school that week, even more than she usually did, except when it came to her history lesson with Mrs Jones, a subject she normally hated with a great passion. She had never seen the point of learning about what had already passed, but today, she took a great deal of interest.

They were learning about world war two, Grace realised that Flo would surely have met with the atrocities of this war later in her life. Grace wished she had taken more notice in her lessons and knew more about it, she was yet to learn that Flo had already lived through the first world war, or as Flo knew it, 'the great war', 'a war to end all wars'. How untrue that turned out to be.

Grace was beginning to comprehend the impact of it all.

Flo would have been in her early 30's when the war started. Would she have survived? A great many people died in World War Two. Grace worked out that today Flo would be about 100 and therefore probably not still alive. She was disappointed, maybe she could have tracked her down, just to confirm that she really didn't imagine the whole thing. She should have asked more, she really didn't know much about her at all. Why had she spent so much time talking about her stupid phone when Flo's life would have been much more interesting.

Jenny nudged her.

"What?" snapped grace.

"Oh, excuse me, when did you become such a swat" Jenny sneered.

"Sorry, I was daydreaming"

"This is so boring" said Jenny.

Grace quickly agreed fearing she would give something away, but of course Jenny would never guess her secret in a million years.

Thursday seemed twice as long as the other days, and net-ball practice seemed more miserable and cold than ever.

Grace and Jenny finally began the walk home. Grace tried to act normally but her stomach was doing somersaults and she could barely concentrate on Jenny's babblings about how much she hated Amy Johnson because Amy Johnson had been chosen to play goal attack, a position Jenny thought she would be much better at and she was sure Amy Johnson got her own way because her mother worked in the school as a mentor and got her special treatment. Grace thought this probably wasn't true and that Jenny was just jealous, not that she would tell Jenny this and, to be honest, Grace wasn't really that interested at the moment.

She so desperately wanted to meet Flo again.

The two girls said their good-byes at the top of Leasowe Road as usual and Grace walked the next 20 yards towards the shop. She checked the time and wondered if the exact time was relevant to their meeting. Grace wanted to make sure she came out of the shop at exactly the same time. 4.54. Remembering how the time had never changed while she was with Flo.

She looked into the window of the video shop to waste a few minutes and then finally she entered the shop, bought a Mars Bar, took a deep breath, checked the time and made towards the door. She tried to focus on going straight home, enjoying her Mars Bar and looking forward to her evening as if to already soften the blow of disappointment.

Chocolate bar clutched and melting in her hand, one last check of the time, Grace held her breath and opened the door of the shop, her eyes half closed, the way you do when watching a scary film.

Chapter 8

1964

Grace stepped out, blurted out a short laugh and immediately clasped her hand to her mouth.

Before her were the familiar sights of old times.

Grinning from ear to ear, she frantically looked round. she saw strangers hurrying past, but no Flo. she stood for a minute or two. she felt elated to be here again but her stomach sank when she could not see Flo.

"Grace" a familiar voice shouted, Grace spun round to see Flo walking out of the shop.

Grace ran and hugged Flo as if she had known her forever but hadn't seen her in years.

"I've never been so glad to see anyone in my whole life, Flo, "

The two girls laughed. They felt much more confident than their last visit when they had both been scared that they would not return home, or worse, that they were dead.

"How are you, grace?"

"I'm fine, how are you?"

"I am very well thank you"

Both girls were eager to get the pleasantries out of the way and bombard each other with questions, but they both fell silent with embarrassment for a few seconds as they realised they barely knew each other.

The girls decided to walk as they talked, taking in their surroundings and discussing the differences they could see.

Grace told Flo about Wallasey Village in 2008. There are so many more houses and buildings than 1964, and, of course, so much more traffic. Sometimes you could barely cross the road without using the traffic lights. The village could get really busy with people as well, especially before and after school as there where three big secondary schools within the village and two primary schools.

Flo couldn't imagine having that many people living here to warrant all those schools and she also needed a full explanation of traffic lights, which she found fascinating.

Flo explained to Grace that there were barely any cars around in 1920, in this village anyway, people still mainly got about in a horse and cart or by walking. There were much fewer houses and the roads were rough and narrower without the pavements that she could see now.

Grace took out her phone to double check that the time had not moved on.

The time remained at 4.54.

Flo asked if she could look at the amazing mobile telephone and was memorised by the electronic digits and the photograph on the screen of Grace and Jenny pulling some unladylike faces, which made Flo laugh. She felt as if she could touch their faces as the picture was so clear.

Grace played the ring tone for Flo,. 'I like big butts and I cannot lie', by Sir Max-a-lot . Grace now wished she had chosen something a little more sensible.

"Wow!" Flo was, once more, amazed and wanted to know how the music came out, and indeed, how it got in there in the first place., She wanted grace to play it again and howled when Grace explained what a 'butt' was.

"I really can't explain it to you Flo, it's very complicated, but if you promise not to ask me how it works I'll show you my iPod"

Flo was intrigued. Grace rooted in her bag, pulled out the small pink square. Flo couldn't imagine what this contraption would do. Grace selected 'Angels' by Robbie Williams, a song she had put on for her mother. Grace thought it would be sensible to not choose anything too current, she didn't want to show Flo too much, too soon and she thought 'Angels' would be a nice gentle start for a girl of Flo's musical experience.

Grace helped Flo to put in the earplugs and pressed play.

Flo gripped hold of the wall they were sitting on as though the music would blow her over. She couldn't decide whether she was more amazed at the song that was playing, or the machine it was coming out of. She was frozen, still gripping hold of the wall for the whole of the song, Grace sat patiently humming along, but she didn't want to sit there while Flo listened to the whole 318 songs on her iPod and so turned it off as Mr Williams finished his story of 'Angels'. She did feel like she was taking sweets off a small child and Grace promised that Flo could listen again later.

Flo was so thrilled with the iPod that Grace wished she could give it to her. However, apart from having to explain to her mother that she had lost it she thought it might not be a good idea to send an I pod back to 1920. She wondered what the people of 1920 would think of the small pink musical box.

The girls continued walking towards Harrison Drive. Grace liked the covered walkway over the shops as they approached Grove Road station. The girls stared in at Betty's Hairdressers at the ladies sitting under the big hairdryers, although the customers where oblivious to the girls presence, the girls still pulled tongues at them through the window. Both girls did not dare admit to each other that if the customers could have seen them, neither would have dared be so rude.

"They look like aliens" said Grace,

Flo told Grace she had never met an alien and was intrigued to know what they were. As Grace hadn't yet met one herself she described E.T. to Flo but did add that she wasn't completely sure they actually existed.

The girls decided to walk past their own houses, only to discover that Grace's house on Sandy Lane had not yet been built and Flo's house on Sea Road had since been demolished and replaced by a more modern Mediterranean looking house.

Grace was fascinated that there was a waste ground on the site of where her house now stood and she stood on the spot where she thought each room would now be, slightly twisting her ankle on a stone in the area which would eventually become her kitchen.

Flo had very different feelings and felt extremely sad as they made their way up Sea Road and she noticed the very different house on the spot were her house usually stood. While Flo liked the look of the Mediterranean style house, she wondered where her family where now, and if they had owned this new type of building.

Grace saw tears running down Flo's cheeks.

"Don't worry its just bricks and mortar," a phrase she had heard her dad use when her mum had been upset when she had not been able to buy a house that she had loved because they couldn't get a big enough mortgage.

"No, is not that. It's just that my parents are probably dead now and where will I have gone?" she asked as if Grace would know the answer.

"Please don't be upset Flo, this isn't now for either of us and we have to remember that"

Grace felt that she should be mature and sensible as she realised that this would be a lot harder for Flo than it was for her. She led Flo away.

Flo had always imagined that her family would become rich and maybe move to one of the larger houses on the Breck, such as Heathbank or Darley Dene. She imagined that they would have many servants and would hold lots of parties in the large ballroom for which Flo would wear beautiful gowns. She would make a grand entrance down a large staircase and all the guests would clap and cheer because she would look so beautiful. At the bottom of the staircase she would see Will looking smart and handsome and he would be looking up at her with his hand outstretched ready to escort her to the ballroom for the first dance. Flo brought herself back to reality and realised that Will would probably laugh at her and encourage her to slide down the banister in an unladylike manner. Maybe that's where her family moved to? This is the dream she decided to keep.

"Try not to think about your family and just lets enjoy this".

Flo agreed and the two girls walked towards the Breck.

Flo would normally look out from the top of the Breck and see a vast amount of agricultural land with small cottages along the other side of Breck Road. Now she saw many more houses and shops and a large school which Grace explained was the local boys school called 'Mosslands', Flo assumed it must have been named after the large house on the Breck called 'The Mosslands'. Grace noticed that the school looked almost new and somewhat smaller than in 2008..

Grace liked what she saw, or rather what she didn't see! Her school. She knew it had been newly built but it was still nice to look at the open space where her school now stood, as if this meant she didn't have to attend. She wanted to go and stand on each square of land which now housed the many classrooms and corridors, she wondered which bit was where the chemistry lab was, this was her most hated room, Miss Pearson was the chemistry teacher whom Grace thought must have been a witch in a former life. Miss Pearson would scream at the class at the drop of a hat, which made Grace nervous, not a good combination when delicately experimenting with hydrochloric acid. Grace didn't actually hate school but there was always something better she could be doing.

Chapter 9

1964

The girls decided to walk back down towards New Brighton. They didn't seem to feel the cold, they didn't know if this was an effect when moving in time or just because they were both still so excited about this new secret life they had found, but they just didn't notice the weather.

As they walked back down Sea Road Flo asked Grace what New Brighton was like in 2008. Grace explained that there was not much there anymore, although they were in the process of building a new theatre to replace the old Floral Pavilion Theatre. Flo knew this as The Pavilion which was a small semi circular open air theatre which stood in the Winter Gardens. Grace knew that the area used to be a very busy seaside town from stories her grandmother had told her.

Grace's grandmother was also called Grace and was thrilled when her granddaughter was named after her. Grace didn't much like her name and would have preferred something less old fashioned, like 'Phoebe' after Phoebe in 'friends'. When she related this to Flo, Flo informed her that Phoebe was a person in the bible and so the name was, in fact, really old.

Grace felt a bit silly.

"I don't read the bible to be honest".

Flo looked at Grace, a look Grace thought meant that she would surely go straight to hell.

Actually the look was more envy at the freedom Grace seemed to have in her life.

"I have to attend bible classes and go to church every Sunday, but then" she added, as if to convince Grace that she did have excitement in her life, "we all go to my grandmothers house for tea. She always makes nice cakes and gives us lemonade to drink".

Grace reflected on her own Sunday's. It wasn't always Frankie and Benny's for tea, and she came to the conclusion that on the whole, her Sundays weren't all that exciting. Her routine often consisted of having a lie in, tidying her bedroom (if she really had to), homework, (if she really had to) watching telly (which she really had to), having Sunday dinner and watching more telly. In the winter months this routine was more common than Grace cared to admit, but she did go out a lot more during the warmer weather. Her mother wasn't a great cook and the only time there where delicious cakes after Sunday dinner was if Mr Kipling had been in some way involved.

Grace didn't see that much of her grandparents as her mothers parents now lived in Wales and her fathers parents lived in Yorkshire.

Grace went on to explain to Flo that New Brighton still had a small fair and a bowling alley with a lazer quest. Flo grasped the idea of ten pin bowling, but the thought of being shot at with a beam of light completely escaped her.

"The outdoor swimming pool isn't there anymore, Flo, it's now a restaurant" said Grace proudly remembering that the outdoor pool had been demolished a good few years back, hence the restaurant name 'The Derby Pool'.

"Actually there isn't an outdoor pool in my time either".

Both girls laughed as they found something in common, a non existent swimming pool.

Grace loved being with Flo. She felt she could just be herself. There was a lot of competition with the girls in school, even amongst her own friends. life was a constant fashion show. Clothes, hair style, mobiles phone were all under continuous scrutiny. Flo thought Grace's school uniform was quite funny and her skirt far too short but it all seemed so unimportant and Grace felt quite ashamed that she had joined in with her friends when they had laughed at someone because of these petty details. They never made these hurtful comments to anyone's face, Grace would never like to hurt anyone's feelings and her group of friends were generally quite nice people however, some of the girls in school could be really nasty.

"Please may I have another listen to the song on your pod?"

"Of course you can," Grace choose not to correct Flo on the name of the contraption.

Grace smiled as Flo, who was more familiar with Mr Williams's song, joined in on the ' 'I'm loving angels instead' bit.

Flo had never heard anything like it, and she loved it.

As the girls walked further on they walked past the very real outdoor pool.

"I wouldn't like to get in there today but it must be great fun in the summer, Grace."

Grace agreed.

Flo had never experienced a swimming pool but had spent many a summer in the sea at New Brighton. Grace had been taught to swim at the Guinea Gap swimming pool and would not swim in the sea for fear of what was lurking under the water. She had seen 'Jaws' and was not taking any chances.

The girls continued on their walk along the prom. There were a few people out walking, some with their dogs, some riding their bicycles.

Flo was still wary of the very fast motorcars driving past, while Grace found it quite strange that there were so few cars around, not just the ones driving past but so few parked outside peoples houses.

"Do you have a car Flo?" Grace had no idea when the car had been invented, 'gosh', she thought, 'I really must start researching some of this stuff!'

"No, but our neighbour Mr Johnson bought one last year and he let my father have a drive of it. We were allowed to sit in the back, it was great fun. My father would like one but they are very expensive and they certainly don't go as fast as these cars."

"You should see how fast they go now Flo, my dad was driving at 90 miles an hour the other week. My mum really told him off".

Flo didn't at all know how fast 90 miles an hour was.

"I don't think its a good thing anyway because people get killed when they drive so fast, maybe they should have kept these old cars". Grace added.

Both girls became very tired suddenly and felt the urge to go home. They both agreed and made there way back to the village. Grace would rarely admit to being tired but this absolute weariness made her wonder if she would make it back without falling asleep. The church clock up the hill on St. Hilary Brow showed they had been out for about three hours. The church had been rebuilt in 1859 in the grounds of the previous parish church of St Hilary which had burnt down two years previously although the original tower built in 1530 still stands today. As they neared the shop the girls were more confident that they would meet again but still feared this would be their last meeting.

"See you next week Grace?"

"I really hope so Flo"

The girls hugged again.

They felt like the best of friends.

Chapter 10

1920

"Did you forget something Flo?" Flo heard the familiar voice of Mrs Powell.

"I thought I'd dropped something, sorry" Flo needed to start thinking of some good excuses if she was to keep popping in and out of the shop. She got the impression that Mrs Powell was already beginning to think she was a bit strange. In fact, that is exactly what Mrs Powell did think.

Flo walked home with a spring in her step. The feeling of weariness had left her as she returned to 1920, via the bakery of course where Mr Finch noticed Flo's exceptionally good mood.

"You had a good day then Flo?"

"I have had a wonderful day thank-you for asking Mr Finch, how about you?"

"Just the usual, although our Harry has come down with a bad cold and couldn't help in the shop today, it hasn't been too busy but I think he might be havin' me on. He complained of a blocked nose and a sore throat but managed to eat two thick pieces of bread and some ham for his lunch, can't be that ill if you ask me.

Harry was two years older than Flo and had always looked pale and thin, as if a light breeze could blow him over, but he had the most beautiful green eyes you had ever seen. Flo didn't feel uncomfortable with him like she did with Mrs Powell's son, in fact she thought Harry was quite sweet really, he was always very polite to Flo, but was very shy and could barely look her in the eye at times. Flo wondered how he would manage when the time came to take over the shop. He really wasn't good with the customers and tended to spend most of his time in the back of the shop only coming out front to bring a freshly baked batch of warm bread.

Flo smiled.

"Poor Harry, I hope he's better soon" she said as she walked out hugging the still warm bread to her chest.

Harry didn't get better and died the following week of pneumonia.

Flo had cried for Mr and Mrs Finch, their daughter had died at the age of three after being kicked by a horse and Harry had been their only remaining child, Flo would swear she never saw either of them ever smile again.

"Hello Flo" shouted her mother,

"Will's waiting here for you, I said he could have some supper with us, we're having stew, will you set the table please"

"Hi Will, how are you?" Flo was bursting to tell him about Grace, the fast motorcars, he would love them, and the pink pod which played the music, the like you have never heard before. She stopped herself once again, she would have to have some proof else he wouldn't believe her. Part of her wanted to take him with her and show him all these amazing things but for now she kept it just for herself.

They ate their supper and then went out to play blissfully unaware that poor Harry would soon close those beautiful green eyes for the last time.

Chapter 11

2008

Grace's week dragged again. She started spending time on the internet researching the 1920's so she would have more of an idea of Flo's life. Grace had seen some stuff on the telly but couldn't get her head around what life was like back then. Did they have aeroplanes, trains or electricity? The more she thought about it the more she wanted to know. She discovered that King George was on the throne at the time and that there were another two kings after that before the present queen Elizabeth was crowned.

Grace read the articles with great interest arousing a passion for history that unknown to her, would shape her future. She wanted to show Flo that she had some knowledge of her time. There was no excuse not to. There was so much information available to her and she knew she should not allow her age be an excuse for her lack of knowledge. Grace found herself in front of the computer even during episodes of Hannah Montana.

Grace walked out of school on Friday, looking forward to the weekend and saw her mother, father and brother sitting in their car over the road. Grace knew something must be wrong, her father should be at work and her brother usually finished school ten minutes later than Grace and besides, her mother never picked them up in the car. She thought it was more healthy for Grace and James to walk to and from school. Grace and James disagreed, especially on a cold winter morning. Grace walked slowly to the car. She didn't want anything bad to have happened and so tried to delay the moment.

'The moment' inevitably came as Grace climbed into the car.

"Grace, we are very sorry, but we have some bad news for you. I'm afraid your granddad has died"

Graces mother's eyes were red and puffy from crying.

Grace looked out of the window at the world trying to ignore the moment that she wished wasn't happening.

They drove silently home. Tears ran down Graces cheeks, she looked across at her brother who was trying to blink back the tears.

Grace didn't see her grandparents very often as they lived in Wales but, when they visited the house had always been cosy, despite the old fashioned and tired looking furniture.

Grace's granddad had always given her and James money to go and buy some sweets and would always ask them to get him some liquorice allsorts.

On the last visit James had joked that he would be sending them to the shop for sweets when they were adults. That would no longer be the case.

Since meeting Flo, Grace was more aware of death. She had wondered quite morbidly on her visits to 1964 how many of the people she had seen were now dead, but losing someone close was a different matter and Grace felt real pain in her heart. What she hated the most was seeing her mother so upset.

Grace took comfort in the fact that if she were able to visit 1964 again her granddad would only be a young man of 28. She wondered if he had lived in Wallasey. She knew that the house that Grace lived in now was once owned by her grandparents and that her parents had bought it from them when they had moved to Wales in 1982. As she now knew, the house must have been built after 1964, she would have to find out where they had been living before then.

The funeral was horrible. Everyone was crying. Grace was given the option of not going but she felt it would be disrespectful to her granddad if she didn't. She wished she hadn't.

Her granddad was buried and the thought of him closed in a box and alone filled her with horror. She couldn't get the image of him lying in a dark coffin underground out of her head, even though her grandmother had assured her that he would really be in heaven.

Grace and James were offered the chance to stay off school the day after the funeral. James was more than happy to accept the offer but Grace insisted on going as she hoped to meet up with Flo again.

Grace's friends and some of the girls she hardly knew were very nice to Grace during the day and Grace had returned their sympathetic smiles .

Jenny asked about the funeral and also how her grandmother was. Grace remembered how difficult it was for her when their friend, Louise's, uncle had recently died and Grace hadn't known what to say. It was later when she saw Flo and burst into tears that Flo had asked, what her granddad was like, she was the only person who did.

"Granddad was very stiff upper lip, that's what my mum says. He didn't like to hug and kiss you but he always asked about school and what I'd 'been up to'. he taught us how to play card games and chess. He wouldn't dream of taking us to MacDonalds or the pictures but he took us to some good places"

"Like where?" Flo asked, encouraging Grace to talk more about her grandfather and wondering what MacDonalds was.

"When we were little" Grace explained, "he often took us to the Tam 'O' Shanters farm to see the animals and then we would walk up to see the windmill on Bidston hill. He would take us crab fishing in the marine lake at New Brighton in the summer, he would bring string and sticks and small pieces of bacon, we would take a bucket with us to put the crabs in. We always had to put them back in the lake before we went home, but we always checked who had caught the biggest one first. He did sometimes take us to museums which wasn't quite as much fun, but some of them were interesting" Grace was smiling at the memories of her granddad, she felt better talking to Flo about him and knowing that at that at this time, in 1964 he would be still very much alive. Flo thought he sounded like great fun.

Chapter 12

2008

Grace was rooting through her drawer looking for a belt to go with her new white jeans when she found her old mp3 player. 'Flo would love this' she thought. She would give it to her, and she made it her mission to download some songs she thought Flo would like before the following Thursday. Of course, she would have to include 'Angels' by Robbie.

The following night she carefully compiled a play list of songs she thought Flo might enjoy. High School Musical (obviously), Girls Aloud, The Wombats. She even chose some of her mothers music which Grace quite enjoyed listening to, more of Robbie, Katie Melua, Norah Jones. Grace could be more selective when she knew what sort of music Flo preferred. Finally, Grace made sure that the mp3 player was fully charged.

Thursday came around again and the two girls met as usual.

Grace handed the mp3 player over to Flo.

'It's like my pod Flo but it doesn't hold as many songs, there's thirty two on there, that should be enough to for now and I can put different ones on every other week when I charge it for you.".

Flo was overwhelmed with gratitude and excitement and must have said thank-you at least twenty times, which made Grace feel that she was never grateful enough for anything.

"I've never had anything so wonderful, but it must have cost a lot of money you shouldn't be giving it to me" Flo had tears in her eyes.

"I don't use it any more and they're quite cheap now, they only hold about 50 songs"

Flo was still most amazed that there was even one song on it and smiled from ear to ear as she listened once again to the wonderful tones of Mr Williams. She would have been quite happy to have just this song on it, she imagined that she would happily listen to it over and over for ever

Grace was also grinning from ear to ear. She couldn't ever remember making someone else feel so happy, it was a lovely feeling, but she insisted Flo didn't spend their whole time together listening to music. Grace explained to Flo that she would have to take it back next week to charge it, as she realised Flo wouldn't have this facility. Flo just nodded. She really didn't understand what Grace meant about charging, she was trying not to ask too many questions about absolutely everything Grace said.

Flo put the MP3 in her pocket and wondered about Will again. If she showed him this music machine he would have to believe her adventures with Grace.

The girls walked down Leasowe road towards the Leasowe Castle.

"Have you ever stayed there Flo?". Grace realised this was a stupid question. why would anyone stay in an hotel right near their home.

Flo laughed. the question was more bizarre than Grace thought.

"No, it's a convalescent home for retired railwayman i don't think they would have me there".

Leasowe castle had been built in 1593 by the 5th Earl of Derby and had been used at times as a family home. it had been derelict for a time in the 17th and 19th century and had housed German prisoners of war as well as retired railwayman before becoming a hotel in 1982,

Grace laughed.

"It's a hotel in 2008, I haven't stayed there but I went in the bar once when we went to watch a play in the hotel grounds."

"It's good that it's still used, it's a few hundred years old you know" said Flo

Grace didn't know, but her interest grew and grew as she spent more time with Flo. She made a mental note to find out more about the history of the castle.

"The lighthouse is still there though" said Grace. Moreton lighthouse stood at the end of Leasowe Road. Grace knew that the lighthouse was quite old

" I don't think that's still used though, in fact, I don't think it still has a light anymore"

"Not much of a lighthouse then !" said Flo.

Grace giggled at Flo's sense of humour. Photo's she had seen from the old days always seem to depict people looking miserable. The fact that they are always in black and white probably didn't help. The girls decided that Leasowe Castle hadn't changed much for either of them and turned to walk back up the road towards the village.

Grace stopped and stared at a woman on the other side of the road who was walking with a large Labrador and had continued walking after the dog had left a large dollop of poo in the middle of the pavement. The woman didn't bat an eyelid or even look around sheepishly to see if anyone had seen the dog do it. Grace shared her mothers disgust about people not picking up their dog's poo as she had, on more than one occasion, had her fair share on the bottom of her shoes.

"She's not picked up the poo" she whispered to Flo. The girls hadn't got used to the fact that they could not be heard and still tended to whisper when they were being less than complimentary about passers by.

"I beg your pardon?" Flo was certain she had misheard.

"She didn't pick up the poo and look at the size of it, it's a whopper!"

"Why on earth would she want to do that?"

"Because you're supposed to" Grace replied.

"She should have put it in a plastic bag and taken it home or put it in the bin"

Flo looked horrified and thought the idea quite disgusting, but then howled laughing.

"Grace you live in a strange world"

"Well maybe, but one where you don't end up walking in poo all the time'.

"I'd rather take the risk than pick it up" the thought of it made Flo shudder.

The girls were always sad to leave each other but Flo was looking forward to listening to her pod that evening and maybe even showing it to Will.
They said their good-bye's once more and entered the shop.

"Excuse me love" Grace turned to see an elderly gentleman with her MP3 player in his hand.

"You dropped this" he handed it to her and she muttered her thanks to him.

"Is that one of those things that plays music?" he asked,

"They get smaller all the time, you won't be able to see them at all soon". Grace felt as if she was being blamed entirely for the advancement of technology. She smiled politely at the gentleman and concluded that Flo wouldn't have been able to take it back with her. It was alright to take it back to 1964 where no-one was able to see it, but she imagined that it would cause quite a stir if anybody had seen it in 1920.

Flo had come to the same conclusion as she frantically searched her pockets.

"You lost something again Flo?" Mrs Powell asked. This girl was becoming very strange.

"Nothing important" she lied and headed home disappointed.

Mrs Powell muttered to her son that she thought Flo would end up in the asylum if this strange behaviour got any worse.

Flo still toyed again with the idea of telling Will even though she now no longer had the proof that she was sure would have convinced him.

Chapter 13

1964

The girls became great friends and spent a lot of time talking about the previous week. It was always a much more interesting conversation than with their usual friends because of the vast differences in the way they both lived.

Grace complaining that her mother had made her load the dishwasher more than her brother had last week prompted a need to explain to Flo what a dishwasher was, although the name did rather give it away.

Flo was amazed once more at the wonders of modern science and wished she could live in a time with all these wonderful machines. She knew her mother would particularly like a washing and a drying machine, although Flo found it incomprehensible how these things worked. Washing was her mothers most hated chore and one she left mostly for Alice to do.

Grace had various scribblings in the back of her school books at Flo's insistence that she draw pictures of the machines so she could get an idea in her mind of what they looked like.

Jenny saw the doodlings of various household objects once and told Grace she was crazy and may need some therapy. The temptation to tell Jenny about Flo was difficult to resist, but instead, she told her that she found geography so boring that even drawing cube like objects was more entertaining. Jenny still thought she was a bit mad.

Flo and Grace saw a lot of the same people on Thursdays but as the nights were getting lighter there were more people around and they seemed in less of a hurry.

Flo was still shocked at the amount of leg shown by the women and felt quite embarrassed by it.

Grace explained to Flo that the mini skirt became fashionable in the 60's and had been fashionable on and off since.

"What if they bend over too far, they could show their undergarments" said Flo mortified at the thought.

Grace howled at the word undergarment, but was not as hysterical as Flo after the detailed explanation Grace had given her of the thong.

"Oh my goodness Grace, I could never wear anything like that"

Grace went on to explain how people were often only too happy to bear all in the modern world.

Flo had an image of people walking down the road naked.

"Ugh, I think I'd rather do without a washing machine and a pod if I had to look at that every day". Grace put her straight about the actual levels of nudity in 2008 and the fact that people didn't generally walk down the street naked.

Flo had herself seen some nudity on a trip to the Walker Art Gallery last summer. Her father had taken her and Will and was pointing out the talents of the artist as she and Will just giggled at the sight of the naked bodies in the picture. Flo's father had looked sternly at them both which was enough to make them behave.

Flo's father had never smacked or struck her but he was strict and one look was usually enough. He was a very respected man in the village and Flo was very proud of him. He had always made time for his children even if he had been very busy at work.

Sometimes Flo's father was called out for an emergency and Flo told Grace of a visit he made to Mrs Smith a few weeks earlier.

Mrs smith had been in labour and the midwife was having trouble getting the baby out.

Flo's father wasn't able to get there in time and Mrs Smith and the baby both died.

Mrs Smith already had four other children and Flo had told grace that her husband was lucky to have his mother living with them to look after the other children while he was at work. Grace was horrified and didn't think there was anything lucky about it at all.

"Why didn't she have her baby in hospital?' Grace asked.

"Women don't go to hospital to have babies Grace, that's for sick people"

"But they might have both lived if they had been in hospital" Grace protested.

"Lots of babies die when they are born, Grace, that's just the way it is". Flo was very knowledgeable in the subject as her father never tried to protect his children from the tragedies he encountered. Not that it would matter if he had, as one trip to the shop and Mrs Powell would gladly give an update on all of the babies born locally, dead or alive.

Grace felt very sorry for Mr Smith and his other children and was glad that things had moved on and that babies didn't die all the time. The only one she had ever heard about was when Grace's friend, Rebecca's, mother had lost a baby last year before it was born, which Grace had found terribly sad.

Chapter 14

1964

Grace was unbelievably excited as she waited for Flo the following week.

"Hi Grace" Flo had liked using the unfamiliar greeting and had tried it out on Will a couple of times.

" What do you mean 'hi' you're not a cowboy Flo" he had said, adding,

"You are a little strange at times". Flo was a little hurt as she was starting to care more about what Will thought of her.

She was finding it increasingly difficult not to give anything away.

"Hi Flo, how are you?" Grace wanted to get the niceties out of the way before she could give Flo her news.

"I'm fine Grace, how are you?"

"I'm great thanks, I've got something exciting to tell you"

"Go on then" urged Flo"

"I'm going to Florida in June. Mum and dad told us last night"

"Where's that then?" said Flo trying to sound excited as well

"Flipping' eck" Flo I thought I was bad at geography. Florida- in America"

Flo's face fell.

"Are you emigrating Grace?" The only time she had ever heard of anyone going to America was to emigrate.

"No, you daft thing it's just a holiday, I wouldn't be excited if I was leaving for ever"

Flo was relieved.

"But you'll be gone for a long time though?"

"Two weeks Flo, just two weeks"

"You can go to America in two weeks, wow you must have some really fast boats"

Grace smiled, she never stopped being amazed at the difference in their lives.

"We're going in an aeroplane" she said as though it were obvious.

Flo looked horrified

"I don't like the sound of that, does your father have an aeroplane then?".

"No" Grace giggled at the thought of an aeroplane parked in their drive. Things hadn't moved on quite that much.

"It's a big one. it holds about a hundred people and you have a qualified pilot to drive it"

"I don't know how they stay up in the air" said Flo

"No, me neither, actually, but they're pretty safe" she said trying to convince herself as much as Flo.

"Anyway, it's going to take about nine hours to get there"

Flo shook her head in disbelief.

"I do hope you will be safe so high up in the air Grace, although I suppose boats haven't always been that safe, there was a big one which sank on its way to America about eight years ago after it hit an iceberg, hundreds of people died, it was really sad. Our neighbours Mr and Mrs Sudworth went on it but we don't know what happened to them, we never heard from them again"

"Are you talking about the Titanic, Flo?"

"You know about the Titanic" said Flo, amazed, as though the girls actually lived on different planets.

"Yes, people still talk about it today. They even made a film about it, you know one of those moving pictures I told you about. My mum loves it , it makes her cry every time she watches it, and I think she probably fancies Leonard de Caprio, he's one of the main characters, but he dies in the end"

Flo didn't think it sounded like a nice film to watch at all.

"It's all such a lot to take in, Grace. Moving picture films, big aeroplanes that take you to the other side of the world in a day"

"Well I wont tell you about the moving pictures on the aeroplane then, that would be just too much, Grace said flippantly. Anyway I'm supposed to be telling you about my fab holiday and we are being morbid talking about people dy(ng on the Titanic. My dad told us about a museum in Florida which has all stuff about the Titanic in and when you buy your ticket it has someone's name on it who was on the Titanic and when you are leaving you get to find out if that person died or survived" she paused to think.

"I suppose that's quite horrible really" she added.

Flo wondered whether Grace would be able to find out what had happened to Mr and Mrs Sudworth. She didn't ask Grace, even if she could find out, Flo wouldn't be able to tell anyone, so she thought it best left alone.

"So tell me about your trip, what are you going to do?" Flo asked more enthusiastically now. Grace always found it difficult to gush about things that Flo would probably never see or do, it always felt like she was boasting, but Flo loved to hear as much as she could about everything. She didn't think she would ever want to ride on a roller-coaster, the speed of the cars she saw in 1964 was enough, but the thought of swimming with dolphins she thought was quite lovely.

"Are you going on holiday this year Flo?"

"We are going to visit my aunty and uncle for a few days, they live in Wales and it will take us about 4 hours to get there by train so I expect you will be halfway to America by then". Both girls laughed and Grace thought that actually she could well be still sitting in the airport after four hours.

Jenny had tried to sound excited for Grace about her trip to Florida but was quite jealous and unlike Flo had barely wanted to know anything about it.

Grace was philosophical about it and felt sorry for Jenny. while a trip to Florida was as likely for Flo as Grace flying to the moon, Jenny's parents were just not able to afford it. Grace tried not to mention the holiday again to Jenny.

"Hey Flo," changing the subject slightly,

"Do you have Wotsits at home?" Grace once again dug into her school bag and pulled out the bag of Wotsits she had taken to school but had forgotten to eat, mainly because two of Grace's other friends had had a falling out and the whole situation took a bit of sorting. She opened the bag and offered one to Flo. Flo looked horrified and so Grace ate one first to prove to Flo, and herself, that they were perfectly safe to eat despite travelling forty four years back in time. They tasted just as good as they usually did and so she offered the bag back to Flo. Flo took one but looked a little doubtful. She put one in her mouth and then screwed her face up in disgust.

"How can you not like them, they're delish"

"They are kind of strange" replied Flo trying to be polite, but wanting to spit the offending Wotsit out and wondering if all the food in 2008 tasted as foul.

"Maybe you just need to get used to them, let me know if you want to try another one."

"Thank you, I will be sure and let you know" Flo didn't think it was likely.

Chapter 15

1920

Flo and Will were walking down to New Brighton. It was Saturday afternoon and the sun was beating down. Flo's mother had given them some sandwiches to take with them and Will had brought a large bottle of lemonade from home to drink.

They often enjoyed summer days paddling in the waters of the Mersey. The sun had brought crowds down to the beach and there were many children splashing in the water having the time of their lives.

They walked all the way along the promenade until they could see across to Liverpool waterfront where they could see the cathedral and the Liver Buildings. Flo had had seen the new cathedral with Grace when they had walked down to the front a couple of weeks earlier and she knew that it had been built for the Roman Catholics. Flo had thought it looked a funny shape, but this was obviously the look of buildings in the future. she wondered how many of the buildings she could see now would be knocked down before Graces time. Grace had told Flo that her father called the cathedral 'Paddy's Wigwam' which Flo didn't think was a fitting name for a cathedral at all. She imagined red Indians running around it making that sound that red Indians make.

Flo and Will walked back towards Fort Perch Rock and onto the sand. Flo took off her shoes and socks, leant back on her elbows and dug her toes into the warm sand. She looked over at Will who was swigging back some of the lemonade from the bottle. He politely wiped the top and handed it to Flo with a smile.

Will was becoming quite handsome these days, Flo thought and she caught herself staring at him for longer than she ought. Will looked embarrassed and jumped up to go for another paddle. Flo joined him. The pair were quite hot and the water was very refreshing. Will laughed as he splashed Flo with the water as though he had never done it before. Flo ran through the water towards him and as Will turned to see where she was he fell backwards into the shallow water. Flo laughed and kicked more water at him.

"Serves you right Will". The water was freezing he was suitably wet and so the pair set off home to Flo's house for tea.

The table was set with pork pies and fresh bread and there was sponge cake for dessert. Will ate as though has had been starved for a week. Flo caught her mothers eye. She was smiling. She liked to see people enjoying their food. Will thanked her for the delicious meal and then offered to play football with Flo's brother after tea while Flo did her piano practice. George idolised Will and sometimes wished he had a big brother instead of a sister. He was sure it would be much more fun. Flo would have preferred to play football but plodded through her scales as expected. She made many mistakes but, nobody knew as they were all busy, her mother arranging flowers in the kitchen and her father engrossed in one of his medical books.

Flo heaved a sigh of relief when her practice time came to an end and she could join Will and George outside where they played until it was dark. Flo waved Will off from the doorstep and watched him walk down the street. She was very happy and hadn't even minded playing out with her brother. She even offered to play a game of snakes and ladders with him before he went to bed.

Chapter 16

1920

"What is that you keep singing?" asked Will. Flo wasn't always aware that more often than not, she seemed to be humming or singing 'Angels'. Anyone else would had been fed up with it by now but Flo loved it. She felt it kept her connected to Grace when they were nearly 90 years apart.

Flo had decided to tell Will about Grace. It had become such a big part of her life that it was becoming increasingly difficult not to slip up and mention her name or talk about something she had done. Flo didn't know whether to try and take him with her without saying anything. That way, if he wasn't able to travel to 1964 with her he would be none the wiser. However trying to make sure he was available at the right time could be difficult.

Will was usually playing football and she thought 'I need you to come to the shop with me Will' wouldn't really sound like an adventure he would want to miss his precious football for.

She wondered if Will would have anything more to do with her if he thought she was mad. Maybe she could pretend it was all a joke.
Her mind was made up. She would tell him before her next visit.

Two days later she met up with Will as usual, she felt nervous and her stomach was turning over.

"I want to tell you something Will but I know you'll think I'm quite mad but please listen and if you don't want to be my friend anymore well that's up to you." Flo spoke without pausing.

"Gosh Flo what have you done, murdered someone?"

"Don't be silly" answered Flo quite indignant that Will thought she could murder anyone.

"I haven't done anything wrong but what I have to tell you will sound unbelievable but, as you are my best friend Will, I am going to tell you anyway"

Will thought Flo must have a good bit of juicy gossip and was intrigued.

"Go ahead then." Will really did want to know now.

Flo wasn't sure where to start and waited a minute while she got it straight in her head.

"Come on Flo, don't keep me waiting", this seemed quite serious.

"I have met a friend called Grace. She's 13, same as us and she's lovely"

Will didn't think this was very exciting at all but let Flo carry on while he tried to look interested in her new friend.

"I'd would really like you to meet her, Will"

"We are allowed to have other friends Flo. It doesn't make you mad. I look forward to meeting

Grace. Are you seeing her this evening? Does she go to your school?"

"It's not that simple" hesitated Flo, "Grace lives in the year 2008"

Will let out an involuntary laugh, 'here's the mad bit he thought to himself.

Flo looked hurt so he tried to look serious and prompted Flo to carry with the rest of her story.

"Grace and I have met up on Thursdays for the past few months and when we meet up it's 1964". she blurted the rest out quickly to get it over with. She tried to read Will's face as he tried not to show his bemusement.

"I want you to try and come with me, but if you can't or don't want to you are quite welcome to call me mad and I shall never speak of it again."

Will wasn't sure whether he should run as far away as possible but found himself asking Flo to tell him more, mainly because she looked so desperate for him to believe her and that she was his best friend.

Flo began to regale tales of her meetings with Grace. She told Will all about the mobile phones, the pod, washing machines, fast cars, aeroplanes, and how they can get to America in just nine hours. Will liked the thought of the fast cars and the aeroplanes.

"That song you keep hearing me singing about angels, well that was on Grace's pod and the man who sings it is called Robbie Williams and he sings in big concerts and makes CD's. Not sure what they are but they are brilliant." Flo tried to remember as much as possible. An hour later Will was still sat quietly listening to Flo asking the odd question to encourage her to go on. It was all a very fascinating story.

Will couldn't quite fathom Flo. It couldn't possibly be true, even he knew you couldn't possibly put moving pictures in a small box in your house or have music on something less than the size of your hand, never mind the time travel aspect, but he wondered how Flo could possibly have made such stuff up. Part of him wished it were true, how exciting it would be to visit the future.

Chapter 17

2008

Grace's brother was having an argument with their mother. He was going on a school Trip for a few days to France and had decided to take his portable DVD player for the long bus journey down. His mother, however, had decided he was not taking his DVD player as he would probably loose it or leave it on the bus. James explained to his mother how careful he could be with his possessions and how much he would pay extra attention to not loosing the DVD player. He even did the tried and tested, stomping up the stairs, all to no avail. Much as Grace loved seeing James not getting his own way she was extra pleased on this occasion and had already decided to borrow his DVD player while he was away and take it to show

Flo. She also knew exactly which DVD to take with her. The times she had danced in her bedroom using her Sing Star microphone, a step up from her hairbrush, imagining she was Gabrielle and singing along with Troy whom she would eventually marry, of course. James would be mortified if he thought that this particular DVD would be played on his precious DVD player. It would tarnish it forever. Grace would point out the time she caught him singing along to 'We're All In This Together' when it was being played on the radio once.

James was less than happy that Grace was smiling through this particular traumatic situation he was in, and she was less than prepared for the cushion which had come hurtling towards her, hitting her right on the face, followed by a barrage of abuse, which ended with 'and don't even think about using it while I'm not here'.

Chapter 18

1920

Flo was really nervous when Thursday came round and had toyed with the idea of telling Will that she had made the whole thing up.

Will turned up at the allotted time and tried to make light of the situation.

"Come on then Flo, lets go and meet your friend then, I want to ask her about the fast cars."

Flo smiled at Will, she could tell he didn't really believe her, why would he? But he was being really sweet about it and she desperately wanted him to meet Grace.

"Its time to go Will"

"Is there a particular time, Flo?"

"Well, yes, we try and stick to the same time in case we miss each other"

Flo knew the situation was sounding more and more ridiculous and just wanted to get it over with. The pair went into the shop and Flo bought another dairy milk bar, she asked Will what he would like. Will chose the same and he wondered what to do about Flo and her fantasy. He thought perhaps he shouldn't have encouraged her, she wasn't the type of person who usually made up stories.

"We don't often see you in here, Will" said Mrs Powell

"How's your family?"

"They're all fine thank you, Mrs Powell"

Flo hoped Will wouldn't get into too much conversation with Mrs Powell. She often kept people talking for longer then they were comfortable with, it was the only pleasure in her tedious life.

Flo had told Will to hold her hand on the way out hoping that this would help her to take him with her.

"Right, is this it Flo" Will held out his hand as they headed towards the door. Flo blushed a little. She was nervous and it felt funny, but nice, holding Will's hand. She had the fingers on the other hand firmly crossed.

As they stepped out she squeezed her eyes shut. She felt the wind on her face and was sure she felt the sensation of Wills hand in hers, but when she opened her eyes and looked round, he was nowhere to be seen.

Flo immediately burst into tears.

"Flo, what's wrong, what's happened?" Graces familiar voice was comforting to Flo, but she cried even harder and it took a couple of minutes for her to calm down and explain.

"Oh I'm stupid Grace, really stupid"

"What have you done?"

"I told Will all about you and tried to bring him with me. It didn't work. what was I thinking? He will think I am completely insane and if he doesn't have me locked up then he'll surely never speak to me again".

Grace hugged her and told her everything would be alright.

"Tell him it was just a laugh and you just wanted to see if he was a good enough friend to believe you".

"Do you think that will work?".

"Of course it will. It'll all be fine". Grace wasn't really convinced herself but didn't know what else to say.

The girls time together was always very precious but Flo was so worried and nervous about going back.

Grace tried to keep Flo amused. She let her listen to her iPod for longer than usual, she asked her if she liked her new t- shirt. It was half term and Flo was more used to seeing Grace in her uniform. Flo loved the t- shirt with Tinkerbell on it, the white jeans with the silver belt, but the pink shoes were her favourite part of the outfit. Graces mum had bought grace the pink converse with the extra money her father had earned doing overtime the previous month.

Grace also showed her the photographs on her phone of a sleep-over she had on the previous Saturday night.

Flo thought it looked such fun. She wished she could have a sleepover with Grace. The girls were all in their pyjamas, most of them pink, and their faces made up with various colours. The girls had also given each other wacky hair styles but Flo couldn't be sure if they were normal or not.

Flo's favourite picture was of the chocolate fountain. She couldn't think of anything more divine, but Grace had left the best 'til last.

"Ok Flo its time to show you the beautiful Zac Effron in action".

Grace had mentioned Zac Effron on more occasions than necessary and Flo had wondered if he could be any more handsome than Will.

Grace pulled out the DVD player already charged and loaded with the necessary DVD. She opened it, placed it on Flo's knee and instructed her to press the play button.

"It's one of those moving pictures Flo, and that is the gorgeous Zac.

Flo forgot about Will for a few minutes and stared open mouthed in amazement at the fantastic pictures in front of her. Despite Grace's previous explanation she never imagined anything so wonderful as this. She did think Zac was quite handsome although they all spoke with a funny accent. Flo had never heard an American accent before, but what fascinated her the most was the dancing, especially the cheerleaders in their matching red costumes.

"Grace this is amazing, it almost feels as though I am there with them" Flo wondered what age she would be when she could see these moving pictures in her own time. She hoped it wouldn't be too long.

The grave reality of seeing Will again soon overshadowed the exciting High School Musical and she asked Grace if she would bring the moving picture box another time, assuming she would not now be locked up in an asylum.

The girls parted once more, with Grace trying to reassure Flo that everything would be ok.

Chapter 19

2008

Grace stepped out of the shop to head for home. She felt so sorry for Flo and hoped Will would be kind to her. She fished in her bag for her iPod and fitted the earphones into her ears for the walk home.

As she looked up again something caught her eye, something not right, out of place.

She looked over and saw a young boy pinned against a wall looking terrified.

Grace couldn't believe it, but she knew straight away, similar clothes and the look of horror on his face.

She went over to him.

"Are you Will by any chance?"

"This cannot be real" he said in total disbelief.

"I didn't believe her, I thought she was nuts, my goodness, are you Grace? is this really 1964?" Will was physically trembling.

He knew it must be because of the fast cars he could see, although he could barely believe his eyes.

Grace couldn't believe it either and was ecstatic.

"Well, I am Grace but this isn't 1964, this is 2008"

"2008" it sounded like a funny number for a year, Will thought.

"Where is Flo?" Will could barely take it In and his eyes darted from one thing to the next.

"She's never been here in 2008, we always meet in 1964, she was trying to bring you to meet me, something must have gone wrong, but please don't worry, me and Flo are quite used to this" she said, sounding quite the expert.

"You'll be alright, you'll be able to go back home" she hoped she wasn't wrong and that the rules of their time travel would be the same for Will as it was for her and Flo.

Despite his heart still pounding in his throat and his mouth being so dry he could barely speak, will suddenly remembered his manners and offered his hand.

"Pleased to meet you Grace"

Grace giggled nervously, she wasn't used to shaking hands with people.

"Pleased to meet you too, Will". Grace couldn't believe it, she was so excited. It was like meeting Flo for the first time but without all the scary bits.

"If Flo hadn't told me all about you Grace I would be sure I was dreaming"

"Well its definitely not a dream Will, I am completely real" Grace said patting her stomach as if to prove it.

"Them cars really do go fast. Flo said they did" Grace wondered what he would make of the motorway.

"How do they go so fast?" it was a rhetorical question he knew Grace wouldn't know, her being a girl and all, but Grace answered confidently

"It's something to do with the emissions". Sunday evenings watching top gear were not wasted she thought, although she was in fact, quite wrong.

Will didn't understand what she meant anyway, but was very impressed with Grace's knowledge.

"They don't look at all safe"

"Well sometimes they're not" Grace answered and left it at that.

Will was transfixed by his surroundings. It all looked so different. Not just different, not just like a place you hadn't been to before. The cars, the buildings, road and pavements

"Is this really Wallasey Village, the same road, the same shop?"

"Yes Will" replied Grace

"What's that?" Will pointed at the traffic lights. He hardly knew what to ask first.

"They are traffic lights. They stop the cars so you can cross the road".

"Wow do the cars really stop for you?"

"They have to, its the law, but only when the lights turn red"

"Its a good job, you wouldn't want to get hit by one of those, they could really do harm to a person"

"Sometimes they do" answered Grace.
Grace became aware of people staring and wasn't in the least bit surprised, Will did look unusually dressed and out of place.

She was trying to think of something to say if anyone spoke to them, but after a while she noticed it was not Will they were staring at, but her.

It suddenly dawned on her that they couldn't see Will, 'they think I am talking to myself' , she thought.

"Will" she whispered, "we'll go somewhere a bit quieter, people can't see you, they think I'm talking to myself. I'll get locked up."

Will thought that would be a bit harsh.

"They wont really lock you up will they Grace?" he didn't know this modern world and anything was possible.

"No, but they will still think I'm mad".

"Grace, can we stop the cars, with the lights?"

Will sounded quite excited and it reminded Grace once again of the thrill of pressing the button and waiting for the green man when she was younger.

Will was suitably impressed by the cars stopping and the picture of the flashing green man which meant you could cross the road.

Will was looking constantly around as he walked, taking everything in.

Grace and Will stopped and sat on a bench. There was a shyness between them. Grace didn't usually just chat to a boy she hadn't met before and despite there being a million things to talk about she didn't know where to start.

It was Will who broke the short silence.

"Flo told me about your pod and your movable telephone"

"Oh, yes, would you like to see them?" she rummaged in her bag and pulled out her phone.

"It's called a mobile phone, you can use it almost anywhere, I'll show you how it works" Time would not stand still while she was with Will as she was in her own time so she had to ring home and explain her lateness. She showed Will how to get the contacts up first. He couldn't understand how it knew what number to ring if you pressed 'home'. He listened as Grace made the call.

"Hi mum, is it ok if I stay out for a bit with Jenny for an hour or two?"

Grace didn't like lying, but what else could she do, this was not the time for truths.

Will was amazed by how clearly he could hear Grace's mothers voice, as though she was sitting next to them.

"Ok love, teas at six, don't be any later".

Will thought Grace smelt really nice as his head was inclined towards hers during the phone call.

"I never would have believed it if I hadn't seen it with my own eyes. I really thought Flo was mad, making all this stuff up"

Next out of Graces bag came the iPod.

"This is my *pod*". she didn't give it the correct name as she didn't want Will telling Flo she had got the name wrong.

Will stared again in disbelief.

"Can it play that song that Flo keeps singing to me, the one about angels?"

Grace rolled her eyes and smiled.

"Flo drives me mad wanting to listen to that song every time we meet, so you can listen to it once, and then I'll play you a more suitable song"

Will recognised the chorus from what Flo had sang to him but was more fascinated by the tiny box of music. Grace thought that despite his rather geeky old clothes Will seemed quite cool and so she selected a more modern song for him to listen to. "Heartbeat" by Scouting For Girls seemed to suit him, although she hadn't thought it through and the line 'she's a pain in the arse' made Will laugh hysterically. Grace thought Will had a knowing look of agreement as if the phrase was an accurate description of all girls.

"I suppose you have to get used to this type of music"

Grace pretended to be insulted

"What do you mean, they're a brilliant band"

"Does Flo like them?"

"I haven't played any of their songs to Flo yet"

"Well I'll consider it a privilege then"

Grace decided Will wasn't worthy of listening to such a good band and so chose '1973' by James Blunt in retaliation.

Grace felt guilty that Flo wasn't with them, it was as if she had met up with Flo's best friend behind her back.

Grace and Will talked for ages. He wanted to know all about the thing Flo had told him, like the aeroplanes, television, fast food. Will couldn't decide which was the most exciting thing. He was less interested in the domestic appliances.

"I suppose they are a good help for the women"

"Actually, things have changed Will" Grace replied indignantly

"Men use them too you know"

Will considered himself told off.

Throughout their conversation Will managed to follow every car that passed with his eyes almost making himself dizzy. He was fascinated by each and every one and desperately wished he could ride in one. He would intermittently want to look at the mobile phone and then listen to a song on the pod. It was almost too much to take in and he could still barely believe it. He would have to eat a large slice of humble pie when he next saw Flo.

Grace knew that Will had lived in one of the houses in Beresford Road, and that the houses were still there, but she wasn't sure if it was a good idea for him to see his house. Will would be 100 years old now, same as Flo, if he was still alive, Grace knew that it was unlikely that Will's family would still be living there and he wouldn't know them if they were, would he? She left the decision to him.

"Would you like to see your old house? it's still standing"

"Wow, really, it must be over 100 years old by now, I'd love to see it"

He had quickly done the maths and found it a bit disconcerting that he would probably not still be alive.

"We won't knock on the door Grace, because if a very old man answers I'll be very worried"

Maybe visiting his house would be too much, thought Grace, until Will added

"I'd hate to think I might of lost me good looks"

Grace laughed and playfully punched him in the arm.

"Flo never told me how modest you were".

"Anyway, just to be serious for a minute, Flo and me decided it was best not to think about what has happened to you or your family"

Grace thought it might be easier for Will as he had gone so much further into the future.

They walked towards the house, Will still watching every car. His favourite so far was a red Mondeo, probably because of the colour. 1920's cars were generally black or grey. so although possibly not Jeremy Clarkson's favourite choice of car, Will thought it was a beauty.

Will was amazed how so much of the surroundings had changed, the roads all seemed neat with pavements and driveways, and every house seemed to have a car outside. Will then grinned as his house came into view.

He thought it looked as good as new. The windows had been changed and the house had been painted cream. Will didn't notice the well established lilac tree, the neatly planted rows of marigolds and pansies, the beautifully laid block paved drive. What he could see was the shiny polished Triumph Bonneville motorbike in the driveway. Will was mesmerised by the chrome and black machine.

"Wow. look at that!" his mouth was wide open. Grace shook her head.

"Will, this is your house in the future and you're more interested in a motorbike" Grace rolled her eyes

"Typical!".

Grace tried to accommodate the needs of her new guest and told him about the egg run. An event in which thousands of bikes travelled together from New Brighton to Clatterbridge Hospital to raise money and take Easter eggs to the sick children.

"There are all sorts of bikes, Will, my dad is always interested in the really old bikes. some of them might be as old as you". Grace wasn't clear on the history of the motorbike.

"That's if you have any motorbikes in 1920" Will put her right. Yes they did have motorbikes but there weren't many around and certainly not in the village, but as soon as he possibly could Will decided he would buy one. He could see himself racing around the streets, especially on one of these beauty's that stood before him now.

"I love it here Grace, how long can I stay?"

"You'll know when its time to go. Me and Flo always know when its time, don't know how or why, we just kinda do"

The feeling had never changed for Flo and Grace, even though they had met so many times and felt safe and confident that they would always get home, they still knew when it was time to leave. A group of girls walked past who were wearing vest tops and skimpy shorts. Wills head faced forward but his eyes followed them as they passed him. They were giggling, three of them with their phones glued to their ears.

"Things really have changed, Grace"

"Don't stare Will, its rude"

"I thought they couldn't see me"

"No, but I can"

Grace looked down at her t-shirt and jeans and felt a pang of jealousy at Wills fascination of the girls.

"Some girls dress inappropriately" she quickened her pace and realised she had sounded just like her mother. She felt silly and turned to smile at Will.

"Next time you see Flo, ask her about thongs"

"What are they?"

"Just ask Flo" she decided not to have that conversation with him, she would leave that pleasure for Flo.

They continued on until they reached New Brighton prom.

"The sea's still here then" Will said

"Did you think we'd have moved it by now" laughed Grace.

Will noted the lack of pier that he so often played on.

"You seemed to have moved most things".

"I didn't move them all myself Will".

They didn't get too far down the prom to observe the Liverpool skyline when Will had the feeling, so familiar to Grace, of needing to go home. They had talked for so long that Will hadn't seen a lot of this new world, but it was enough to be going on with. They walked back to the shop. Grace had butterflies in her stomach.

"I hope you can come back Will its been really nice to meet you"

"I really hope so Grace and I'll certainly try. There's so much more to talk about and see. And its been really nice to meet you" he added.

He reached out to shake hands with Grace but she instinctively stepped towards him and gave him a brief hug. It was a brave move for Grace but she did it in case she never saw him again.

Will smiled and blushed.

"Good-bye Grace".

"Bye Will."

Will entered the shop and was gone.

Chapter 20

1920

Mrs Powell was used to Flo's strange comings and going in the shop and now Will was at it too.

"You forgot something Will?' she asked

Will was caught off guard.

"Er, yes, er, no, nothing, thanks, sorry, good-bye Mrs Powell" Will was flustered and got out of the shop as quickly as possible.

Mrs Powell thought he should spend less time with Flo. Maybe they had started putting something in the water which was making the children act strangely, which was a little ironic as Mrs Powell's son was probably the strangest of them all.

Once outside Will could see the familiar figure of Flo a few yards ahead.

"Flo" he shouted, "Flo, wait". Will was more puffed out with excitement than running the 30 yards after Flo.

Flo turned to see Will chasing after her. She blinked back the tears and wished she didn't have to have the inevitable conversation with him, she felt stupid enough without him seeing her crying.

She couldn't pretend she had made it all up, she had gone too far. She cursed herself. No matter how fond she was of Grace, why did she do something which could cause her to lose her very best friend.

Will was grinning from ear to ear. Flo's heart sank.

"Please don't laugh at me Will, I know you think I'm stupid and mad and I made all that stuff up but I don't want to talk about it, I just want to go home. I'll understand if you don't want to be my friend anymore, I'm just a silly girl and you are better off hanging around with the boys". The thought of this was unbearable but Flo would understand. Flo had hardly paused for breath so Will waited until she had finished.

"First of all Flo, I don't think you're stupid or mad, well not more then usual anyway, and secondly, I did meet Grace, I really did"

Flo couldn't work him out. Why was he saying this? was he trying to be nice or was he humouring her.

"You didn't come with me Will, you didn't meet Grace, but thanks for being nice anyway"

Flo was cringing, she just wanted to go home.

"I didn't go with you Flo, because I met Grace in 2008, in her own time"

Will sounded so excited but Flo looked at him in disbelief.

"Really I did Flo, honestly. I'll prove it. She was wearing a pair of some funny looking trousers which she called jeans, some funny pink shoes made of material and a t shirt which had a fairy on it, you know the one from the Peter Pan story"

Flo felt like crying all over again with relief.

"Tinkerbell" she blurted

"That's her! and she had hair cut all different lengths which finished at her shoulders, Grace, not Tinkerbell, funny looking, but kind of nice though"

"You should have seen it Flo, the cars, wow, they really go fast and there was a motorbike, really big and shiny as new".

Will continued to tell Flo of his visit to 2008 with such enthusiasm, barely pausing for breath, including a detailed account of the shiny new bike and the red Mondeo. Flo listened to every word, sharing Wills excitement.

She wondered why he had met Grace in her own time but she never had and although she was really pleased for Will, a very small part of her was a little jealous. She had wanted to let Will share in a part of her adventure, but he seemed to have had one all of his very own.

Chapter 21

2008

Grace was thrilled to have met Will, she thought he was lovely. It was exciting to see Wills reaction to all the things he hadn't seen before and she would recall the look on his face for a long time to come.

The temptation to tell Jenny about Flo and Will was even stronger. It wasn't just a secret between Flo and Grace now Will was involved and because Will had been able to come and see her, maybe she could take Jenny with her, although would Jenny end up in Flo's time? She decided she still wasn't ready to share her new friends, this was her adventure and her's alone.

Grace did feel bad for Flo, she knew Flo would be happy that Will would at least believe her but she also knew she would be disappointed that the three of them hadn't been together and that she hadn't been able introduce Will herself.

Grace looked forward to Thursday more than ever and really hoped she would meet Will again, she wished the days would go by twice as quickly as she usually did.

Grace had already been told off twice in maths and French for staring out of the window daydreaming. Mondays were always boring and Grace didn't feel good that morning. She had a niggling pain in her tummy which seemed to be getting worse. Maybe she needed the loo. The pain became really intense that she hardly dared to breathe, She became hot and sweaty and the colour drained from her face. She put her hand up to attract the attention of Mrs Brown and then promptly vomited all over the desk, with some slight spotting to Lucy Jones blazer and Jessica Howells pencil case.

There was the generally expected reaction of 'urrgg' from her fellow classmates who, on mass, moved to the other side of the room in disgust and with complete disregard for Graces health. Mrs Brown was equally disgusted but rushed over to Grace to comfort her and asked one of the other girls to go and fetch help from another teacher.

Grace felt terrible and didn't look so good. After a prompt phone call from her mother she was whisked off home with her head bowed into a carrier bag. She just about managed to mutter her apologies to Lucy and Jessica.

The pain was getting worse and the cool flannel her mother had placed on her forehead felt quite soothing but frankly wasn't making her better. Grace didn't recall much about the car journey to the hospital and the doctor prodding her tummy, just to be sure it really was as painful as it seemed. She didn't recall hearing the diagnosis of appendicitis and the discussion about needing surgery, or her mother crying at the side of her bed, because 'she didn't want to see her baby go through this'. She just woke up feeling whoozy and a little sore but relieved that the dreadful pain had gone.

All was now well and the nurse persuaded Grace's parents to go home and return the following day. She assured them that Grace would be well cared for.

Grace took in her surroundings and the other children in the ward, some of whom were tearing around and didn't look like there was anything wrong with them at all, some looked a little more unwell, not least the little girl opposite who looked painfully thin and pale. Grace wanted to ask the nurses what was wrong with her but didn't want to appear nosy. The poor girl lay staring into space. Grace wanted to cry for her and hoped she would get better soon.

Grace was allowed home the following day with strict instructions to rest for a few days.

She had already resigned herself to the fact that she would not be able to meet Flo or Will this week, but she was desperately disappointed, the thought of waiting an extra week was almost as painful as her appendicitis, but not quite.

In the few months that the girls had been meeting they had only missed seeing each other on two occasions. The Easter holiday that Grace had gone to visit her grandparents and the week that Flo's mother had insisted she accompany her on a trip to Liverpool to buy Flo some new boots, which also included a visit to Flo's aunt and cousins in Everton for tea, but both girls had known these arrangements in advance. This time there was no way of letting Flo know. She imagined how she would feel if Flo hadn't turned up to one of their meetings. She looked at her mobile phone. On this occasion it was of no help to her at all.

Chapter 22

1964

Grace, now fully recovered from her ordeal came out of the shop with her fingers crossed. She hoped Flo hadn't given up on her since she had not turned up the week before.

Flo appeared and hugged Grace harder than ever.

"Flo I'm so sorry I wasn't here last week I had to have my appendix out last Monday and wasn't able to come"

"You had your what out?" although appendectomy's were performed in the 1920's they were not common and it was certainly something Flo knew nothing about.

Grace explained what it was and what was involved in the procedure. Flo was amazed at the neatness of the scar.

"I cant believe you're even out of hospital never mind out of the house"

Flo's father had visited many of his patients in the hospital after they had operations and they seemed to be in for weeks. She also knew an awful lot of them didn't survive. So she was especially glad to have Grace back and healthy and hoped she would never had to have another appendix out.

After the gory details of Grace's operation the conversation turned to Will.

"So you met Will then?" said Flo.

"Yes but I'm sorry you weren't with him Flo, he's really nice and funny like you said, although he was mainly interested in the cars and bikes"

"Yes, I know, he hasn't stopped talking about them since, but he thought you were nice too Grace"

Grace blushed a little and wondered exactly what he had said about her.

"I'm sure he would have liked me better if I'd had wheels" she laughed.

"Did he try to come with you again this time?" Grace asked trying not too sound too keen. She sensed Flo's slight unhappiness at them not all being together.

"He tried to come with me again but he hasn't appeared"

They both knew this could mean that Will could be waiting for Grace when she returned to 2008, Grace was hopeful and Flo a little jealous. Flo had known that there would be little she could do to stop Will returning to see Grace, not that she wanted to but she had hoped that this time he would be here in 1964, she felt a little left out.

Grace had missed Flo and savoured her time with her but really looked forward to the possibility of seeing Will again.

"That woman is a bit strange" said Grace

The middle aged woman, dressed in a smart green suit with a fur collar, was leaning against her new MK 2 Jaguar smiling.

"She's been stood there grinning since we arrived"

"She looks quite posh" Grace was glad to steer the conversation away from Will.
Flo thought she looked familiar. They must have seen her here before.

"Maybe she's waiting for her lover" said Grace

"Grace, really" said Flo pretending to be shocked.

"Well he must be quite nice by the smile on her face. Shall we wait and see?"

"No, its a nice evening, there'll be lots of people on the prom, I like to look at their funny clothes" she said looking Grace up and down. Grace was wearing white jeans and a Mickey Mouse t- shirt.

"Cheek of it, what's wrong with this?" Grace had thought she looked quite cool today.

Flo laughed,

"Nothing, you look really nice actually."

Chapter 23

2008

Grace had struggled with a dilemma since taking notice in her history lessons and learning all about World War Two. did she tell Flo about it or not? What would Flo do with that information? She tried to imagine herself in the situation. Who would believe Flo at the moment? And when it came to nearer the time what would you do? Would you move to a safe place? Where would that be? A remote part of the country that would be unlikely to be bombed, would you move to another country? Who would you take with you to save them from the war? Your close family, extended family, friends, neighbours, their families, where would you stop?

Grace mentally made a list of the people she would want to help.

Mum and dad, brother (maybe!), grandparents, aunts, uncles, cousins, Jenny, her other friends. The list would spread like a chain letter.

Grace didn't know too much about how the war affected Wallasey and although she knew she could find out, she decided not to, for now at least. That way her ignorance would lessen the guilt she would feel, and although still a child, Grace knew enough to know that you can't or shouldn't change the past.

Grace had nearly slipped up when Flo had mentioned the great war on a previous occasion, which had lasted from 1914 to 1918. Grace had nearly asked if she meant the 1st or 2nd World War, Grace hadn't known in what year they had both taken place at the time. It would be awful to think that Flo would spend the next 19 years dreading what was to come instead of looking forward to her future.

Chapter 24

2008

Grace and Jenny walked home as usual and were accompanied by three boys who had come to know Jenny through playing football at the weekend. One of them, Paul, fancied Jenny and found her particularly attractive as she shared his love of football and especially his beloved team, Everton. Grace rolled her eyes at his blatant flirting which Jenny was falling for and reciprocating. One of the other boys, Luke, became quite interested in Grace and made a valiant attempt at flirting himself.

"Where do you live, Grace?" he really was quite sweet but Grace wasn't interested, she was just looking forward to meeting up with Flo and maybe Will again.

"Oh, further up the village" she answered flippantly, she didn't want to give too much away for fear of him stalking her.

"I really am in a rush, though" the poor boy took this as a big fat 'I'm not interested in you' and coolly acted as though he didn't care.

"Ok see you around then". Grace did feel a little sorry for him.

"Yeh, see you", "bye Jen" she shouted past him,

"See you tomorrow"

"Bye Grace". Jenny was not at all bothered by the lack of Grace's company on the way home today, she was very much enjoying the attention she was getting.

Grace quickened her step to break away from the testosterone filled boys and half jogged her way to the shop. As she came to Leasowe Road she looked back to see them far in the distance and continued on her weekly mission to meet Flo and hopefully Will.

She stepped towards the door of the shop and pushed. The door didn't move and so she pushed a little harder, still the door didn't move. She stepped back and scanned around the door as if to try and find where the fault lay. She stepped back even further and noticed the large sign in the window, the sign that made Grace's heart sink, which read 'closed for business, we would like to thank all our customers past and present for their loyalty'.

Grace felt herself inwardly panicking. She felt sick, she really had to get inside. She peered through the glass to see if anyone was inside, but the shop was mostly empty and dark.

'Oh my god', she muttered to herself. she felt completely helpless. 'Flo will be waiting for me' she thought. she didn't know what to do.

"I think its closed Grace". Luke had caught up with her. Grace was flustered.

"Oh, I just really fancied a Mars Bar"

"Is that why you were in a hurry?".

"No, I was just going to run in quickly".

"There is another shop up the road which I think sells Mars Bars, shall I come with you"

Luke thought he might as well give it one more go with this very pretty, if a little strange, girl.

'Another shop' she wanted to scream at him. Another shop won't do.

"No thanks, never mind, I really do have to get home, sorry"

She ran home in tears.

Grace tried to think logically. surely they would open another shop within the next week or two, and it wouldn't matter what they sold she would still go in, and then she would explain to Flo what had happened, yes, that's what she would do.

Almost every day for the next four weeks Grace walked past the shop and peered in through the window looking for signs of refurbishment, but the shop remained as it was.

Grace felt devastated, she desperately wanted to get a message to Flo, but how could she? She wondered what Flo would be thinking and hoped that she would realise there was a problem and that Grace couldn't help the situation but would see her as soon as she could.
However this was not to be.

Grace wasn't sure how many times she had peered in through the shop window for signs of life. Four months later Grace stood over the road in front of the school and watched in horror as the demolition firm tore down the small block of shops, after a fire, which had been started by some local boys who had broken into the empty shop. The fire had destroyed a large part of the building. It would be six months before the rebuilding started to create a new premises for a local vet, and on the site of the much loved shop would be space for parking.

Grace cried herself to sleep once again. She really was grieving for her friend and didn't know whether she would ever find her again.

Chapter 25

1964

Flo was now also wondering if she had lost her friend. She had realised there must have been a problem and that Grace would not have just abandoned her. She had prayed that nothing awful had happened to Grace.

That first day, Will had gone too, hoping to meet Grace again. he had held onto Flo's hand, a little more tenderly this time. He had squeezed his eyes shut and with his heart thumping and his mouth as dry as a bone he stepped out of the shop. His heart had sank. There, was the familiar sight of the Travellers Rest, and old Mr watts going in for a pint or two, who then usually managed one or two more.

Flo had wandered up and down waiting for Grace. She knew after half an hour that Grace wasn't coming and returned home. She wondered if maybe she was in hospital again having another appendix out.

Flo too visited the shop every week for months. The novelty of 1964 had worn off without Grace's company. She was used to the same shops, buildings and cars, even the same faces of the people walking up and down. There was no appeal anymore and she never stayed more than half an hour, waiting and hoping. Will would go with Flo as often as he could hoping maybe he could get through to 2008 again, but he never did.

It would be another 75 years before Grace would even be born.

Chapter 26

Flo loved the view from her bedroom window, the views across the Welsh hills were beautiful. She liked all the different shades of green and yellow of the fields. She would watch the birds swooping down for food and sometimes, her aunty pegging out the washing in the garden. There was little else to look at though and Flo was bored. She spent her days reading, sewing and sometimes helping aunty with some light chores. The days were long she felt very lonely as she looked out. She missed her family, she missed WIll and she still dearly missed her friend Grace.

As time had moved on she was resigned to the fact that she would never meet Grace again, it was as though Grace had died. At least her own family where only 50 miles away in Wallasey and she knew she would see them again soon.

She had had a strong belief that she and Grace would meet one day in heaven but in her current predicament, she felt she would surely go straight to hell.

She would know nothing of what the rest of Grace's life had been like.

Flo was, at present, staying with her Aunt Jane in Wales. as she approached the ninth month of her pregnancy she loved the feeling of her baby squirming in her tummy, but cried every day at the prospect that this baby was to be taken away from her and adopted.

Arranged by her father, the couple in their thirties who had not been blessed with their own children, Catherine and Frederick, where anxiously waiting for their new baby to arrive.

It was her father who had realised that Flo had been pregnant. He had seen the swelling in her belly as she had reached up to a cupboard. He had dropped the cup he was holding. He had seen enough pregnancies in his time to know. Flo's mother had spent the next week crying.

Catherine and Frederick Burgess lived in Wallasey, although Flo was led to believe that they lived in Wales.

Flo knew her parents were only doing the right thing and they had been gentle with her. They had told her that she was too young to have such responsibility. They had played down the shame they felt about their daughters condition and suggested she live in Wales until the birth claiming that the air would be better for her. Friends and neighbours were told that she was suffering from pneumonia which had left her weak, although some had their suspicions, not least Mrs Powell who had not kept her thoughts to herself!

Flo knew from conversations with Grace that in years to come it would be perfectly acceptable to keep her baby.

She remembered when Grace had told her about the girl in school who had a baby when she was only fourteen and was allowed to go back to school whilst her mother cared for her baby.

These were cruel times, after all, Flo and Will were very much in love.

Will would write as often as he could. He missed Flo as much as she missed him, and was overwhelmed by guilt and shame. It really hurt him to know what she was going through and that he couldn't be there to help and support her. He had wanted to run away with her but he knew that this couldn't have been possible.

Flo's aunt walked in with some tea to find Flo crying again.

"There there child, stop all this nonsense, there'll be plenty of time for babies when you are married. Her aunt had never had children, she didn't understand, Flo wanted this baby. Her aunt left the tea on the dresser and went to start dinner.

Flo cried all over again.

Chapter 27

1923

Flo was woken by the pain which made her want to double over, impossible with her swollen belly. She instinctively blew out through pursed lips until the pain subsided. She didn't then dare move or breathe in case the pain returned, which of course it would. Next time the pain came she was more prepared, but it was no less painful, she cried out to her aunty.

Her mother had been due to arrive the following day, a week before her due date, Flo needed here now, more than she had ever needed her as a small child when she had scraped her knee or had a nightmare.

Her mother, however was several hours away, even if she had been easily summoned, and this baby was not necessarily going go wait for her.

Flo's aunt ordered her husband to fetch the midwife, this would take a good hour and in the meantime the role of midwife would be played by the unwilling and terrified aunt, who had no clue what she was doing.

She fetched towels and laid them on the bed, wondering if there were enough to save her old and worn but perfectly serviceable mattress. She hoped Flo's instinct would take over and that she would deliver this baby herself. Many woman had done the job perfectly well on their own. The baby did wait for the midwife. Another six long and painful hours. The midwife told them they had called her far too soon and had wasted a lot of her time today, although she didn't seem to mind the constant supply of tea and more than adequate lunch that was provided for her.

The midwife had no qualifications to speak of but had nine children of her own and had been delivering a large amount of babies in the village for the past 20 years. She had witnessed a lot of joyous occasions and more than enough tragedies. She had also delivered her fair share of illegitimate babies. She had little sympathy for these unmarried mothers and didn't easily hide her feelings, but they had all needed her and each one hoped she would be able to take away their pain.

Flo couldn't bare the pain and did not understand how anyone would go on to have any more children, even though she knew many of the women in her village had several children, a lot of them unplanned and unwanted.

Flo's aunty had felt increasing maternal instincts as she had watched Flo's belly swell. She wondered whether she should have offered to adopt the baby herself, but it had already been promised, and she knew that Catherine and

Frederick would shortly get the long awaited news that a healthy baby girl would be soon be ready for them to take home.

Catherine had been preparing the nursery for months. Fred had tried to persuade her to wait until the baby had safely arrived, but the walls had been painted a pale yellow and a hand crafted mahogany cot had been placed in the corner of the room. There was a hand made quilt which Catherine's mother had appliquéd with little ducks in anticipation of a long awaited grandchild.

Flo got to keep her baby for a full week before it was deemed well enough to make the journey from Wales to Wallasey, this was one of the most precious weeks of her life.

Flo had called her baby Grace, after her beloved friend. She suited the name and Catherine had decided to keep it. Although she didn't really approve of Flo's situation she had felt so grateful to Flo for providing her with such a beautiful little girl that she wanted to respect the name Flo had chosen.

Catherine and Fred would soon make the journey down to collect the baby girl.

Catherine was overcome with excitement and could barely sleep the night before the journey. Neither could Flo.

Flo hadn't cried this much the night she was whisked away to Wales, pregnant and further away from Will than she ever wanted to be.

Chapter 28

1964

Flo, now 57, dressed in a smart green suit with a fur collar, matching heeled shoes, her hair recently permed and styled, stepped out of the new MK 2 Jaguar, and stood staring at the sweet shop. Flo had done well in her business and had travelled to many different countries, but this small shop was, indeed, still one of her most favourite places in the world.

There were people going in and out of the shop and Flo stood and smiled. She recognised some of the people going in for their usual cigarettes and newspapers, but Flo waited. It was Thursday March 12th 1964, quarter to five. She had wondered for some years whether this was something she should do, but right or wrong she wanted to be there. she knew she would not be able to see the two happy innocent young girls but she knew they would be able to see her.

She waited about twenty minutes until she knew that they would have passed her and then walked slowly towards Harrison Drive, taking in the surroundings that had become so familiar, and recapturing some of her precious memories of Grace.

The girls had tried everything to keep a reminder of each other. Apart from the MP3 player which refused to move across times, Grace had taken a picture of Flo on her phone but there had been nothing but a blank screen. They had tried to capture their voices on the answer-phone but still nothing was saved. Grace was sure she would be able to take Flo's ribbon back with her in the hope that as ribbons had existed in 2008 it would be no problem, but the ribbon remained in 1920. and so the girls were only left with their memories.

Chapter 29

2013

Grace stood in the school hall. She had the same sickly anticipation she had felt two years earlier collecting her GCSE results.

Her teachers had known that Grace had become an exceptional student and Grace had been thrilled with the 11 A*'s on the slip of paper. Although her teachers were equally confident about her 'A' level grades, she still had a niggling doubt.

As the students around her were whooping and high-fiving with joy, some crying with joy, others with disappointment. Grace just smiled .
There, were the predicted five A's in print in front of her.

"What did you get Grace as if we didn't know?" Grace showed Jenny the slip of paper.

Jenny was genuinely pleased for Grace, if a little envious, as she looked at her own two C's and a D. Grace had worked really hard and deserved it, and Jenny now wished she had too.

For the few months before their exams, Grace would only generally go out on Saturday nights. Jenny and the rest of her friends thought she was mad. Grace always had a great time when she was out and had made up for it once the exams were over. She had become quite stunning and received a lot of attention from boys. She found most of them shallow and didn't really give them a chance and anyway, she was quite happy trawling through heaps of history books.

Jenny had told her there wouldn't be any more history left to study if she didn't slow down. Grace knew that she had now secured the place at Oxford University and couldn't wait to start the course she had chosen studying history.

Jenny couldn't think of anything worse than more studying and had taken a job in a local building society. She wished she had Grace's ambition and brains and hoped that, although Grace would be moving away, they would remain good friends.

Grace knew that her love of history and her ambition was all down to the time she had spent with Flo and she still missed her greatly.

Grace's parents were incredibly proud of her and Grace tutted that afternoon as her mother sat leafing through her address book to make sure she hadn't left anyone out in her quest to tell most of the world about Grace's results.

The family were going out for tea to celebrate that evening and Grace had chosen to eat at a 'two for one" restaurant.

Her brother who was currently studying engineering at Lancaster university, still had one more year to go and Grace knew that her parents had been struggling to help him financially over the previous two years. She knew that it would be more difficult for them with both her and James at uni and she hoped one day that she would be able to help them out, but for now choosing a "two for one' restaurant would have to do.

Chapter 30

1926

Flo loved the view from her bedroom window, it was the same view she had seen since she had been tall enough to look over the window sill.

It wasn't the best view in the world, looking over a neighbours garden at a line of washing blowing in the breeze, Flo had watched Mrs Smiths undergarments getting increasingly larger over the years. Her parents had the room which overlooked the sea.

Although it was autumn, today the sun was shining and everything was beautiful because today was the day Flo and Will were to be married. Flo had finally reached the age of 18 last and her father had given his consent for them to be married. He had, when he discovered Flo's pregnancy, told Will he was no longer welcome in their house, but had mellowed over time as he realised how devoted Will was to Flo and although they had been totally devoted to each other for the previous four years he had made sure they waited until they were eighteen.

Flo's parents had never spoken of her pregnancy since the day she returned from Wales. To them it was as if it had never happened, hence they were happy for her to marry, in white, in a church. Perhaps to prove to the gossips that, of course, the rumours had been untrue. Mrs Powell was disgusted, but was still happy to take their money over the counter with a smile.

"Flo, are you awake?" her mother brought a tray of tea and bread with jam.

"I don't think I could eat a thing, I'm far too excited"

"Now listen here my girl, I don't want you fainting halfway down that isle in front of your father and spoiling that lovely dress. Now then you eat up and I'll get your bath ready, I'll put some of those nice bath salts in it, you know, the ones your father bought me for Christmas last year"

"Thank you mum, I'll eat the bread"

Flo looked over at the beautiful lace dress hanging on the picture rail. She had brand new white stockings and undergarments.

Flo giggled to herself at the thought of wearing one of those thongs that Grace had told her about.

Flo would still carry a small cloud of darkness with her even today, her two Graces, as she had come to think of them, her baby and her friend. She had mourned the loss of both of them and over time she had put them both in a separate box in her mind. Although she thought of them both often, she had learnt to carry on with her life. She recalled the many good times she had shared with Will and the day she had returned home after four long months to find that he still loved her as much as she had loved him, although she had returned without their beautiful baby girl.

Today though, was a happy day. Flo was so excited, but managed to eat most of the bread, despite the butterflies in her stomach.

Flo looked at herself in her mothers long mirror.

"Wow, I look quite beautiful" she thought to herself. Will thought the very same thing.

Chapter 31

2013

It was during the summer after her "A" levels that Grace started her research, she thought it would be good practice for when she went to uni, so she set about applying for birth and death certificates and searched the census. She wanted to trace her own family tree, but first she searched for the long awaited proof of the existence of Flo. Grace did not need to prove to herself that she had met her a few years before but she longed to see something in black and white.

Grace soon had in her possession a birth certificate.Florence Elizabeth Renshaw born 23rd September 1908. Tears rolled down Grace's cheeks as she stared at the certificate. She felt as if she now had a real connection with Flo.

Next, Grace searched and found the wedding certificate of Florence Renshaw and William John Davidson dated 20th November 1926. Grace gave a short burst of laughter and cried all over again. She felt so happy for them both as much as she would if it were their wedding day today.

Grace trawled and trawled, but found no trace of any children born to the couple. Now she felt the chapter completely closed. Grace had hoped to find Flo's children and grandchildren and had imagined so many different scenarios. Would she just see if there was any family resemblance, would she befriend them somehow and get them to talk about Flo or would she tell them everything and risk them thinking she was not of sound mind. Now the decision had been taken out of her hands and the happiness she had felt for Flo and Will was tinged with sadness at the thought they had not had any children. Grace wondered if they weren't able to or if they had decided not to. She hoped that they hadn't been put off by finding out what life was like in the future.

The final certificate Grace had applied for really did make her cry and although she knew that Flo would have long since died, to see the death certificate of her friend with whom she had laughed and shared so much with just five years earlier was overwhelming.

Grace did not feel as much emotion whilst researching her own family tree as she had never known these people as she had known her beloved Flo.

Three of Grace's grandparents were still alive and so she worked back from there.

On her fathers side, Grace managed to trace some of his ancestors back to Ireland in the early 1800's and then on to Liverpool, possibly as a result of the potato famine in the 1840's which led to a very large proportion of the Irish emigrating, many of them to America.

Grace's grandmother on her mothers side whom she was named after was brought up in Wallasey village.

Grace Elizabeth Burgess was her maiden name, born on 8th march 1925.

Grace was surprised to find that she had been adopted and though she was intrigued as to why, she discovered after more research that adoption had not been legal before 1926 and were usually arranged privately. This meant that Grace would be unlikely to find information on any blood relatives before this. She decided that there was little point in researching her adoptive parents, Catherine and Frederick Burgess, as they were not blood relatives.

Chapter 32

1987

My dearest Grace,

I don't know how you would ever receive this letter but I am writing to you in my 80th year and you will be born in 8 years time.

I would have loved to have met you again but my health is failing and I will certainly not be living another 20 years.

I wanted to tell you about my life and to wish you love, luck and success in yours.

Although I only knew you for a few short months I considered you my best friend and was privileged to know you.

I have had a good and happy life I will start by telling you that Will and I fell in love and I became pregnant at the age of 16. We were unmarried and my parents decided that it would be best to have my baby adopted.

I had a beautiful baby girl and she was adopted by a couple I knew only as Catherine and Frederick. I named her Grace, after you.

I think about my daughter every day and always wonder what her life was like.

I prayed one day she would wish to find me, but as time moved on I realised this was more and more unlikely and I fear now it is too late.

Two years after having my baby, Will and I married but unfortunately were not blessed with any more children.

My dear Will was killed in the war at the Normandy landings in June 1944. He was only 36 years old, I still miss him every day.

My own family survived the war despite Wallasey being badly hit during the blitz, but then my dear brother George was killed in a car accident aged 44, with his dear wife and son. I never remarried, not that I wasn't asked of course, but I never could replace my Will. And I was so glad that you met him.

At the end of the war I decided to train as a solicitor and I bought some property. I knew from our conversations that this would be a good investment. It gave me a comfortable life and I have travelled the world, have met many wonderful people and have made some very good friends.

I really enjoyed watching the world approach 1964 and beyond, seeing all the things appear that I had already seen or known about such a long time ago.

I live in London now but have returned to Wallasey on many occasions to see all the developments take place, and also to bring back the memories of our meetings.I hope you enjoy life as I have done and I hope that one day you will find your own Will.

Yours, Flo

The letter, which lay in Flo's bureaux was never read. With no family left, Flo had left her estate to various charities and friends and the house was cleared by a company who would discard the letter along with any other seemingly unimportant documentation.

Chapter 33

2020

Grace loved the view from her bedroom window. It was a beautiful view over the Caribbean sea. The view had taken Grace's breath away when she had arrived three days earlier, but today the view was especially beautiful as this was the day she was to marry Charles.

Grace had met Charles at university where he had been studying economics. Grace had thought him a bit snobby and posh at first but her initial impression had been wrong and she soon realised how sweet and kind he was, and how much he adored her.

They had chosen the beautiful island of Barbados to have their wedding ceremony, and as Grace looked out onto the calm blue sea she wondered as she did often, particularly when something significant was happening in her life. 'What would Flo think of it?'

Grace and Charles's parents had come over for the wedding, as had Grace's brother James, who had given up calling Grace an idiot long before she had attained a first in her history degree at Oxford

A couple of Charles and Grace's best friends from uni had also come over for the wedding. Grace hadn't wanted a big wedding and so it was easier to have it abroad with very few guests. She had invited Jenny, although they weren't as close since Grace had moved away. Jenny had declined the invitation for financial reasons but had wished them all the luck in the world.

Grace had chosen a simple long ivory dress with which she would wear some very pretty gold coloured flip flops. She would wear her hair long and loose with the ends curled and she would have a small gold locket around her neck, Which she had been given for her 18th birthday by her parents.

Despite the simple look she had chosen, Grace looked stunning and Charles had tears in his eyes as she walked towards him. Her mother cried throughout the whole ceremony.

Chapter 34

2021

Grace didn't get back home too often. She saw her parents every couple of months as they had more time on their hands. They loved visiting Grace and would often see a show while in London.

This week Charles had gone away on a conference and so Grace decided to go back home for a few days and catch up with everyone.

She had arranged to meet up with Jenny on the Tuesday afternoon. They would go to Liverpool, do some shopping and have a long lunch. Thursday morning Grace woke early with the sun streaming into her room. She spent the day with her mother, they walked along the prom in New Brighton and had lunch in another new café which Grace hadn't seen before, the place seemed to get busier every time she returned home. Whenever she came home she would always have a walk round the village. The memories of when she met up with Flo always seemed stronger than her other childhood memories and she never want to loose them. She would shut her eyes and recall the 1964 village she had loved.

As she got to the bottom of Sandy Lane she couldn't help but grin. On the site of her beloved shop there now stood a newly built Tesco express. She was surprised her dad hadn't mentioned it. He would have said they were taking over the world. Grace hardly dared to hope that she could go back and see Flo after all this time but, what if she could. What would it be like if she met the 13 year old Flo now she was 26? She would certainly give it a go. She wandered up and down until the appropriate time, she felt a bit silly but who would know?

Finally, she stepped into the shop and, feeling more self conscious as she had got older pretended to look disappointed as though they didn't have what she had come in for. She stepped outside with her eyes closed.

Grace stood open mouthed. She knew the feeling of stepping into another time, and initially felt excited and hopeful that maybe Flo would be here too, would Flo realise who she was? What would she make of a 26 year old Grace, but as she looked around, Grace could not possibly even guess at the year she had arrived in. She put her hand slowly to her mouth, and with tears in her eyes, she looked around at what could only he described as a ghost town. There were no signs of life at all. There were no cars driving or parked. And the buildings were derelict. Grace turned to look at the new Tesco store she had come out of and saw an empty shell with rubbish strewn on the floor. The windows had long been broken, but by what or by who? The village felt eerie and Grace shivered. She hadn't wanted to see this but it was too late. How much more did she want to know? What year was it? Just how far into the future had she travelled Grace looked around for clues but there were none. The rusted sign of St Mary's Academy gave no clue. A lot of the buildings had changed. The row of shops opposite the school had been knocked down and replaced by a large hotel which had been built to service the many more visitors to New Brighton. This now looked old and shabby.

Why had everyone deserted this place which had become so popular in the 2020's.

Grace was terrified. She wanted to run back into the shop and pretend she hadn't seen this, but she had.

Grace didn't know whether to search for more clues to find out what year it was. This could be hundreds of years in the future, of maybe much earlier than that. She wondered about her parents. Maybe the people had just moved away for some reason. Grace's worst thought had been nuclear war, but surely the buildings would have been affected. Instead they just looked old and ignored. Grace didn't know how long she had stood there. The clock on St Hilary's church didn't help, although it was still standing it had long since lost its hands.

Grace knew if she left now she would be tormented by curiosity. And although she felt, and was, completely alone she decided to walk a little. Grace approached the top of Leasowe Road. The roundabout at the top which was usually decorated with neat rows of bedding plants now looked like a small island, full of overgrown bushes. The trees had pushed their roots through the roads. Grace noticed birds, lots of birds, seagulls. As she walked she could hear a familiar sound. A very familiar sound but misplaced. And as she appeared at the top of Leasowe road the glinting caught her eye first and then the source of the familiar sound. The lapping of the tide coming in, right up to where the petrol station had stood and across as far as Grace could see.

Grace now stood on the very small island of Wallasey. The sea had invaded her home town. She walked the other way and up the hill. She stood in the grounds of St Hilary's church, behind her, buildings were empty but still standing, in front, beyond Breck Road where her school had been and the boys school had been and where Jenny had lived, the tide was moving in. There was nothing but water, the lighthouse with no light long since washed away.

The people had gone, chased away by the tidal waves that had intruded their home town. Grace was mesmerised. After a few minutes she ran back to the deserted shop her heart beating fast and fingers crossed that this wouldn't be the time that she could not return home.

She felt a huge sigh of relief as she heard the familiar sound of beeping as someone's shopping was loaded into a bag for life by a cheery shop assistant. Grace walked quickly to the back of the shop and stared into one of the freezers as she tried to compose herself. The checkout girl asked Grace if she was OK. Grace was white as a sheet and felt sick. She wanted to tell the shop assistant and everyone she passed what she had seen, but instead she bought a newspaper and left the shop. She arrived at her parents home and ran upstairs to her old room where she cried uncontrollably. Her mother appeared at the doorway and asked what was wrong. Grace couldn't tell her.

What would be the point?

for

Tom Jack and Megan

6505865R00127

Printed in Great Britain
by Amazon.co.uk, Ltd.,
Marston Gate.